TOM J. FATJO, JR. used to be a quiet but efficient accounting executive. Then one day in 1966 he bought a garbage truck — and started an amazing adventure. In the next 10 years Tom and his associates built Browning-Ferris Industries, Inc., the world's largest solid-waste disposal company, with 1980 sales in excess of $550 million. And that was just the beginning. Since 1974 he has been a founder of Mortgage Bank, which after 2 years was servicing more than $400 million in mortgage loans, and Criterion Capital Corporation, whose subsidiaries and affiliates manage over $2 billion. In addition, he has been instrumental in building 9 other companies ranging in sales from $1-200 million. This is Tom's first book.

KEITH MILLER, who spent 15 years in the oil exploration business before becoming a writer, is one of America's most popular authors on personal guidance. His bestselling books include the modern classic, *The Taste of New Wine*, along with *A Second Touch*, *The Becomers*, *Habitation of Dragons*, and *Please Love Me*. Keith's other coauthored books include *The Edge of Adventure*, *Living the Adventure*, and *The Passionate People*, all with Bruce Larson, and *The Single Experience*, with Andrea Wells Miller. Among his other speaking and writing activities, Keith has been a consultant to The Houstonian, a renewal center developed by Tom Fatjo for executives and their families.

Recapturing Your Dreams
Through Creative Enterprise

WITH NO FEAR OF FAILURE

Tom J. Fatjo, Jr. & Keith Miller

WORD BOOKS
PUBLISHER
WACO, TEXAS

First Key-Word Printing — October 1983

WITH NO FEAR OF FAILURE: Recapturing Your Dreams
Through Creative Enterprise
By Tom Fatjo, Jr. and Keith Miller

ISBN 0-8499-4168-7
Library of Congress Catalog Card No.: 80-54807
Printed in the United States of America

CONTENTS

ACKNOWLEDGMENTS

Many people helped us with the content and preparation of this book. A number of friends read all or part of various drafts of the manuscript. But Dub Duff, Lynn Gavit, George Harris, Russ Harris, Vester Hughes, Tom Luce, Bill Martin, Roger Ramsey, Tom Tierney, Bill Walker, Arthur Wang, and Bob Waters took the time to give us detailed responses and suggestions which were invaluable.

Laurie Casner, Judy Filer, Joan King, Mary Jo Palmer, Pam Richard, and Patty Smith did the typing and/or kept us moving forward on the book (and everything else we were doing) during the writing period.

We are grateful to all these people, to Word editors Floyd Thatcher and Anne Christian, and to the others at Word who gave us valuable criticism and encouragement. We didn't take all their suggestions, so we can't blame them for any errors that appear in these pages. But we are very thankful for their help.

Special thanks go to Tom and Doris Fatjo for a lifetime of help and support for their son, Tom. And finally, we want to thank our wives, Judy and Andrea, those two entrepreneurs who have loved us through the rewrites (and who have both started their own business ventures since we began writing). It is to them that this book is dedicated.

FOR THE READER

—From Keith Miller

When I was a little boy I imagined I was going to accomplish something special someday. And I dreamed about what I might become. I didn't know if I'd be an outstanding ice skater, actor, businessman, or writer. But I felt sure there was something great out there with my name on it.

I am convinced that hundreds of thousands of Americans felt that way as children. Unfortunately, though, when many people grow up, they either leave their childhood dreams behind or bury them in the basements of their unconscious minds. But some men and women don't get over those feelings or dreams of a special destiny. And it's out of that pool of adults who still remember their dreams that the creative ventures of tomorrow will rise.

If you recognize yourself as one of these people, then—whether you are young or old, and whatever your color or sex—we believe you are a candidate to join the coming wave of realistic dreamers who will fulfill their dreams and aspirations.

Tom Fatjo and I are writing to men and women who are restless and are seeking career changes, to entrepreneurs or others in midlife who are rethinking their own lives and goals, to people in corporations who might be interested in a dynamic development process which can dramatically increase sales and productivity. We are writing to people taking on a career for the first time, to students getting ready to begin, to homemakers who want to develop a dormant area of their lives, or to people who have been through divorce or have retired and need to start toward new goals. We are in fact reaching out to *anyone* who is dissatisfied with the quality of life he or she is experiencing in the midst of an affluent, changing society, and who would like to take a serious shot at fulfilling his or her dreams.

Since the sixties, many people who rebelled against the notion of "being controlled" have left the streets and "gone into business for themselves," or they have taken jobs in corporations and brought a new spirit with them. Because of the changing tax structures and increased governmental regulations, those men and women have had to learn new and creative ways to build businesses and fulfill their larger vocational dreams. And, quietly and surely, they have.

What has been happening, it seems, is that, in the shadow of a growing tendency toward bureaucracy and seemingly contradictory or unnecessary governmental controls, America has been spawning a new generation of innovators—a new breed of entrepreneurs. These new movers and shakers often have a low profile, and tend to be very realistic about financial numbers as they plan and dream.

One of these innovators is Tom Fatjo, Jr., around whose story this book has been written. Before he turned forty, in 1980, Tom had accomplished the following:

(1) Beginning with the purchase of one garbage truck in 1966, he started a company that became the largest solid waste company in the world—Browning-Ferris Industries, Inc., a major New York Stock Exchange corporation with 1980 sales in excess of $500 million.

(2) In 1974, he was one of the founders of Mortgage Bank in Houston, Texas, which after two years was servicing in excess of $400 million in mortgage loans.

(3) He is chairman of Criterion Capital Corporation, a private investment firm which he founded in 1976, and whose subsidiaries and affiliates now have over two billion dollars under management.

(4) In 1977, Tom founded and became president of The Houstonian, a $39 million project dedicated to creating a more productive quality of life. It opened in January of 1980.

(5) In addition, Tom has been instrumental in the formation or development of eight other companies ranging in annual sales from one to two hundred million dollars each.

I met Tom Fatjo in the fall of 1979. As I got to know him, I began to see that he is not only an example of a new breed of entrepreneurial giants, but also a man who has discovered a deceptively simple creative process through which difficult vocational and personal goals can be accomplished. And I saw in Tom a man who has applied that process to his own life in a way which has brought a great deal of simplicity and happiness into what could be a complex nightmare of demands and commitments.

Since my own personal and vocational experience had been a mass of overcommitments and stress for some years, I decided to try Tom's process in my own life. And in six months the experience of peace and relative simplicity, accompanied by a new sense of direction and control of my vocational life, was so dramatic and encouraging that I put aside my own writing schedule to work with Tom on this book.

Since Tom's process for venturing came out of his own experience as a businessman, I urged him to begin by telling something of his own vocational life and experience. Although he did not want to do this, he agreed in order to clarify what is said later in the book.

Not long after we started writing, I began to see that the creative process we were describing and the people who use it are, or could be, a very powerful force for social change. So I want to confess that there is embedded in these pages a dream Tom and I share. The dream is a picture of America as a giant Rip Van Winkle, waking from a long sleep and coming alive again to lead the world in productivity and the reexperiencing of a creative and healthy quality of life for all kinds of people who want to work for it.

It seems ironic, but somehow very appropriate, that the man who developed a process which might help people find a better quality of life and clean up some of the social messes we've gotten ourselves into learned the process as he was busy becoming the largest disposer of garbage in the world.

Since this process has changed my own life profoundly and

opened new horizons for me and my family, I hope this book will be helpful to you.

KEITH MILLER

P.S. The following pages grew out of discussions between Tom Fatjo and me. Tom dictated the basic body of material; I shaped that into a book and added several chapters based on our common experiences and understandings. The book from this point on is written in the first person singular from the perspective of Tom Fatjo.

FEAR OF FAILURE AND THE DRIVE TO SUCCEED

The title of this book, *With No Fear of Failure,* could suggest that I am a courageous person. Actually, I've always been afraid that I'm basically a coward. And yet I have hoped people would see me as being courageous.

All my life I've known men and women who have seemed to demonstrate amazing confidence. Some athletes, when interviewed before a game, absolutely "know" they're going to win. And I have talked to ordinary businesspeople, attorneys, and outstanding entrepreneurs who always appear to have great confidence in themselves. But it just hasn't worked this way for me. I have a lot of doubts and fears about failure.

I recall vividly two incidents that occurred when I was a boy which affected the rest of my life deeply, and which may shed some light on my reasons for writing this book.

One night I had a date with a girl who had been my "steady" a year earlier. On this particular evening we were double-dating with another ninth-grade couple, and we went to a little country dance in a small town nearby.

Since we'd quit going steady, this girl had been dating someone in the twelfth grade. Several of this older boy's friends were at the dance, and they looked us over as we came in. I felt uneasy, and my date seemed embarrassed that she was with me.

During the evening, a couple of the older fellows danced with her. Then, when it came time for us to leave, one of them held on to her hand and wouldn't let her go with us. I felt my stomach tense and my heart begin to beat faster as a wave of fear swept over me. I really couldn't tell whether she wanted to leave or not, but I was afraid to force the issue, so we walked outside without her. My friend, Kenneth Oshman, his date, and I waited in the car, assuming she would come along. But she didn't. Finally Ken said, "We've got to go get her."

I was frozen to the car seat. Even though I was an athlete and prided myself on being a football player, there was just no way I could bring myself to go back inside and stand up to those bigger guys. But even though Ken was small and not particularly aggressive, he got out of the car and headed back into the building where the dance was being held. In a few minutes, much to my amazement, he calmly walked out of that place—and my date was with him.

I cringed inside with shame—and still do every time I think about that evening. I knew then that I would always have to pray for courage, and I have.

The other incident took place when I was nine years old. I was playing in a sandlot football game on the schoolyard in Richmond, Texas. A big boy three years older and a foot taller than I came charging down the field right at me. I was the last one who could tackle him and keep him from making a touchdown. He looked huge, and I felt scrawny and very scared, yet I wanted with everything in me to tackle him and save the day.

As he was bearing down on me, the runner was smiling—he knew I was scared half to death, and he was going to run right over me. But then, somewhere in my imagination, I saw my dad's eyes looking at me intently, as if to see if I had the guts to tackle that big guy. Suddenly I felt a surge of energy; I gritted my teeth and charged forward. My shoulder hit him so hard it knocked the breath out of him, and we both fell to the ground. I can still see the surprised look on his face as he lay there gasping for breath. But I was a whole lot more surprised than he was.

Somehow these two scenes are parables of my childhood years. The combination of the desire to be a strong man and accomplish great things on one hand and my fear of failure on the other has driven me to look for an approach to life and to business which would open the way for an aggressive effort to achieve large goals while at the same time reduce to a minimum the risks of failing.

In thinking about people like me—people who want to fulfill their vocational dreams in spite of the fears of failing or looking foolish, the words *venture, entrepreneur, enterprise,* and *innovator* come to mind, and I have used them continually throughout this book. While these are familiar words to most of us, I'd like to take a brief look at their definitions. (1) A *venture* is "an undertaking involving chance, risk, or danger." *To venture* is "to proceed despite danger." (2) An *entrepreneur* is "one who organizes, manages, and assumes the risks of a business or enterprise." (3) An *enterprise* is "a project or undertaking that is especially difficult, complicated, or risky." (4) An *innovator* is one who introduces changes (or makes them happen).*

When I use these words here to describe myself and you and the exciting prospect of recapturing our dreams, I am using them in a broader sense than they are ordinarily employed in business.

For example, I have a friend, Frances Baxter, who was at one time a national Latin dance champion in the United States. According to Frances's husband, her commitment to dancing was all-consuming. After reading an early draft of this book, Frances said, "The characteristics you set out as those of a successful entrepreneur remind me again and again of those I had to live by and cling to in order to have a career in dancing." Apparently, the inner qualities necessary for success in totally different vocational fields may be very similar. "Maybe," Frances commented thoughtfully, "we can all have an opportunity to become entrepreneurs!"

I believe that what she was saying is true. In our complex and confusing world I've talked to many people who are dissatisfied with where they are and what they are doing. Their minds seem to be caught in a swirl of conflict. Some would like to

---

* Definitions are from *Webster's New Collegiate Dictionary,* 1973 ed.

leave their jobs and go off on their own vocational adventure. Others dream of concentrating their efforts and abilities on changing things in the context in which they already live or work. But I'm convinced that most of us are afraid to go after our dreams because we don't know how to begin or how to set new goals and do the kinds of thinking and planning which assure the best chance of succeeding.

Everyone who starts a new venture—whether a Charles Lindbergh carefully planning to cross the Atlantic, a Henry Ford launching an infant industry into the mainstream of world transportation, or a homemaker deciding to go back to school or start a business—faces certain fears, inner struggles, and temptations to quit. But there are ways of planning and of handling adversity and setbacks which have often made the difference between those who have risked and succeeded and those who have never really begun.

That's what this book is all about. I want to share here an approach to setting goals and planning which can, hopefully, lead people beyond the fear of failure so they can achieve personal fulfillment and success. This book is about the process of dreaming—and about moving your dreams out of the safe harbor of speculation into the deeper waters of success and failure.

The book is in four sections. The *first* describes something of my own experience in helping build a business out of which I discovered the process of creative enterprise. The *second* section describes the process itself. The *third* section deals with my own discovery of how the art of creative enterprise can apply to personal living in order to create a healthier and more productive quality of life. The *fourth* takes a look at an approach to solving some of society's larger problems in the free enterprise system.

In describing the creative enterprise process itself, I will often refer to specific Browning-Ferris Industries (BFI) experiences. Consequently, some of my comments may seem self-serving. I have struggled with the fear that I might come across as some sort of egomaniac. But, I have decided to go ahead in spite of my fears. The only authority I can turn to in addressing the problems and opportunities in our system comes from my own adventure as a businessman. If your background is not business you may find a few of the descriptions of BFI organization and development too detailed, but it seemed necessary to include these since the *principles* of the creative enterprise process—which apply to anyone—came out of these years. So, based on my experiences, I hope to convey something of the process I'm discovering, but at the same time I want to share some of the excitement I feel about the opportunities each of us has in America today. And while many of the illustrations I use are taken from the organization and operation of a business, the principles will, I believe, apply to most other kinds of vocational and even personal ventures.

I am aware that my experience differs from that of many people in several important respects. Because of my accounting background and conservative temperament, I sometimes may seem more inclined toward careful planning than many outstanding business builders I know and respect. So I want to state clearly from the outset that I realize this book represents only one of many views concerning what it means to be an entrepreneur. And, as you will see, there are times when I have jumped out and taken risks which would fit the usual stereotype of an entrepreneur. But, again, this book is not really about entrepreneurs in the normal sense of the term. Rather, it is about ordinary, everyday people who would like to move out and capture their dreams.

As we set about to build Browning-Ferris Industries, I made some surprising discoveries which for me were more life-changing than the corporate and financial success we were going after. Because of the intensity of the effort, I became aware that the foundations of my personal life and relationships were being shaken, and I was forced to reexamine my own experience—the ways I actually lived in the different compartments of my life. And the search for physical well-being, simplicity, and peace led me into a whole new style of living.

This is the way it began . . .

PART ONE

The Adventure—Where the Process Came From

Chapter 1

STARTING AT THE BACK DOOR

The garbage was almost up to my armpits in the dank heat of the enclosed truck bed as the driver slowed for the last stop on the route. I shook my head and smiled at myself as I tried to find a clean place on my rolled-up sleeve to wipe the sweat out of my eye. What was I—Tom Fatjo, Rice University graduate and the president of the company which owned this truck—what was I doing up to my chest in garbage?

* * *

A couple of the people at the emergency meeting at the Willowbrook Civic Club that night were really irritated.

"Collecting garbage at the back door can't be *that* complicated!" one of them was saying with a very red face.

Our subdivision in the southwestern part of Houston, Texas, had hired a private company to collect our garbage, because the city would only pick it up at the street or alley and not at the back door. But now the private company was having serious problems, and our garbage was stacking up.

As president of the subdivision, I suggested that we might buy a garbage truck and provide our own service. Silence. Then another angry man said, "Tom, this is a civic club, not a damn garbage company! Why don't *you* buy a garbage truck and be our garbage man?"

I smiled.

But after the meeting that night I went home thinking about what the man had said. At first the idea seemed funny—me, Tom Fatjo, the garbage man in our suburban community. But there was something about it that appealed to me. Since I was a kid I'd wanted to be a physically strong man and had enjoyed being a part of teams or groups of strong people. Long after my wife and daughter had gone to sleep I lay awake, thinking.

At the time, I was a partner, with two other men, in a growing accounting firm. For several years, I'd been evaluating companies for possible purchase and/or for management purposes for my clients. My suggestions were being followed, and large sums of money were being invested on my advice. I felt successful at my work and felt good about what I was doing. But when I was alone, I had begun to experience a deep and growing restlessness. Here I was making crucial decisions regarding the conducting of larger and larger business enterprises, and yet I had never been through the "test of fire" in building a business of my own. (I wasn't thinking of our accounting firm as a "business.") At first I had dismissed the thought of starting my own business, but then I had found myself becoming increasingly curious about possible business opportunities.

But on this particular night while lying in bed, I was suddenly fascinated with the idea of being a garbage man. I had always assumed (correctly) that garbage men are typically big, strong-willed, and volatile individuals, the type of men I had always been a little afraid of—and wished I were like. I'd seen them operating the heavy trucks around landfills and always noticed them as they worked their way up and down the streets.

I felt a growing desire to overcome my fears and to be a part of a tough group of men. As I tossed in bed that night I fantasized throwing the garbage cans up into a truck. I felt strong and earthy and—like a real man.

I got up quietly so as not to waken Diane, and walking past our daughter Kim's room, I went into my study. After moving Kim's baby shoe out of my chair, I sat down and stared out the window at the high, white moon. At first my thoughts were confused, but then I began to play with an idea on paper—the idea of buying a garbage truck.

At the time we were living on $750 a month. My partners and I had agreed when we started our accounting firm to conserve by living on reduced income, so I could certainly use some extra money. Increased income and solving the subdivision's garbage problems were my goals. Next, I listed the financial information I would need to see if going into the garbage business would be feasible. I daydreamed some more about being a garbage man, and laughed out loud as I pictured the look on people's faces when they heard that conservative Tom Fatjo with the white shirts and dark suits was driving a garbage truck. But excitement about doing this was much deeper than the allure of doing something different. I didn't know exactly why, but this crazy idea was suddenly very important to me.

My thoughts flashed back to my college days—all those years of trying to prove myself and never feeling I could quite make it.

I pictured again the Rice University campus on the day I took the entrance examination. I could see the stately red brick buildings, the tall oak trees, and the beautifully manicured lawns. It was the epitome of tranquility, but I was anything but peaceful. Rice is known in the Southwest as a tough school scholastically, and I wanted very much to be accepted academically in order to play football. Somehow the drive to prove myself as a man was wrapped up in my making the Rice team. But my stomach was in knots because I was sure I couldn't pass the entrance examination.

The fear began to build up inside, and by the time of the exam I was so scared I felt like I was in a dense fog. When I got into the examination room, I had to dry my palms on my jeans in order to even hold a pencil. Every question looked ominously foreign and impossible. I panicked, sat there in a cold sweat—and failed. But because of my capabilities in both football and golf they allowed me to begin classes. However, I wasn't awarded a scholarship, and I had to make the required grades to be eligible after my freshman year.

Three years later, just before my senior year, I looked back on what had happened in college with the same uneasy feeling of having failed to really prove myself. While I had done well in accounting and only fair in my other subjects, I hadn't been able to do much in sports.

During my sophomore year I received a call from my dad one day which changed my plans completely. He was a successful car dealer in Richmond, Texas, but severe financial reverses made it very hard for him to continue sending money to me. I'd always thought of my dad as being impervious to failure, so his call was a tremendous shock to me.

Later I was able to understand what had happened—he'd gotten overextended and didn't have the capital to bail himself out. But at the time it only meant to me that I would have to go to work if I wanted to stay in school. Diane and I were planning to get married, so I put sports aside and concentrated on getting through college while working part time for an accounting firm in Houston.

Now it was the spring before my senior year, and I knew the next fall was my last chance to make the Rice varsity. I'd taken a light academic load and played a little junior varsity football the year before, so I went to the coach's office and asked him whether he thought I could make the varsity. Coach Jess Neeley looked at me and smiled.

"Fatjo," he said, "You're not the best center that's ever come to Rice, but then you're not the worst either. You're six-one, you weigh 190, and you're strong. So it's up to you. Come out if you really want to."

Granted, that's not a lot of encouragement, but this was my last chance. I decided I'd go for it and worked hard during the summer to get in the best physical condition possible. At the last of the summer I ran so many wind sprints the week before practice started that my feet were bleeding from the broken blisters.

I'm not sure Diane or her mother ever understood how much I had riding on making the varsity football team at Rice that year. My mother-in-law dropped hints constantly that made me feel I was not being responsible as a married man, since I was playing football rather than working. (Diane had a job, and I had decided not to work during the season.) But I felt somehow that this was my last chance to show what I could do in sports.

Finally, the day before practice started, I went in and checked out a uniform. The smell of sweat and pine oil disinfectant floor sweep brought back a thousand memories—and fears of failure.

After I'd put the uniform in my locker I walked across the campus and sat down on a bench under the tall oak trees. People were passing by, but I was only half-conscious of them.

My feet were so torn-up from doing wind sprints that I could hardly walk. And my heart ached with a deep sadness—I was that nine-year-old kid again, trying to prove he was a man so the world would approve of him.

Then that paralyzing fear hit me again. My stomach tightened. Looking down at my throbbing feet, I felt sure I'd never make it. Maybe I *was* being irresponsible. After all, I *was* married, and I *should be* working.

Within a few minutes I couldn't tell the rationalizations from the common-sense thoughts. I felt sick. I was afraid to go on but afraid to quit. Good Lord, how was I ever going to amount to anything?

I never showed up for practice the next day—or ever. . . .

With a shudder I brought my mind back to my study and the present. No wonder I was fascinated at the idea of making it in a business dominated by big strong men. Deep down inside, I was still trying to prove something to myself.

I stayed up much later that night, juggling figures, making plans—dreaming about the future. By the time I went back to bed, the first rays of dawn were casting a pink tint across the Houston sky. It was the first day of September, 1966. I fell into bed and slept like a baby.

When I woke up at nine o'clock that same morning, I realized I hadn't set the alarm before I went to bed. And I had an appointment with a very sophisticated and prim banker at nine fifteen! As I reached for the telephone, I remembered my "daydreaming" from the night before, and smiled at the thought of saying to my banker friend, "Dan, I'm thinking about becoming a garbage man."

That day I was able to get the financial information I needed and discovered that, with an initial investment of $500, I could earn, after expenses, $2000 to $3000 a month from the operation of one garbage truck and still keep my position in the accounting firm. I had no capital except the $500, and I was very much afraid of being undercapitalized because of what had happened to dad. But I believed there were unusual circumstances which would make this deal fly.

The subdivision had allowed the previous collector to prebill them for three months. That would pay our expenses from the start. And I found that I could purchase a demonstrator garbage truck for $7000 with a note from the bank. It certainly looked as if I had stumbled into a very good opportunity. (What else I'd stumbled into I was soon to find out.)

The idea still seemed outlandish. But as I began investigating the garbage collection business I really got excited.

No one seemed to think the idea was a good one, except my dad. He had moved to Houston and at that time was a car salesman at a dealership near our subdivision. He offered to assist in overseeing the operation and to help me keep the truck in shape. With his encouragement, I decided to risk it.

By the time I made the commitment in my mind to "go" on the deal, I was sure I would not turn back regardless of what happened. All my fantasies of being a star athlete, of succeeding in business, and even of being a garbage man seemed to come together to produce an amazing sense of desire to succeed in this venture. Inside my mind, once the commitment was made to build a company, I decided I would pay *any* price that was ethical and legal to reach my goals. I was sick of my tentative commitments and indecision about going for things I wanted in my life. We decided to call our company American Refuse Systems—quite a name for a firm with only one truck!

Since the garbage problem in the subdivision was so urgent, everyone cooperated, and a few days after the Willowbrook Civic Club meeting I got up at five in the morning and drove the garbage truck to the south end of the subdivision, where I was to meet the helper I'd hired to empty the cans in the truck. We were to pick up the garbage twice a week. I was excited, and it seemed to me that the metallic smell of the early Houston mist was like a strange perfume being worn by destiny. I was on my way!

After we had picked up the garbage at about two hundred homes, Bill, the helper, came around to the cab. "Well, that's it, Mr. Fatjo. The truck's full up."

"It can't be! We're not even half through!" My pencil and paper calculations (made after consulting another garbage operator in Houston) had indicated that the truck we bought would hold the garbage from about seven hundred fifty homes. But it was full after two hundred. My calculations were crucial for the economics of our company's success, and they were off by over 200 percent!

This error in calculations could be disastrous. A round trip to the dump would take an hour and a half. But there was nothing to do that day but make the two extra trips and get all the garbage picked up.

I was very late getting to work at the accounting office that morning and was worried sick by the time I got home in the early evening. I could see now that we'd have to start picking up the garbage at about two thirty in the morning in order to finish before eight. I also realized that our expenses would be 50 percent higher and would eat up the three months of prepayments in sixty days.

I'd done it again. But this time I remembered two things. The first was an incident which occurred the summer between my sophomore and junior years at Rice. I'd decided then to take a light academic load the next fall and try to play junior varsity football. The coach had said that if I wanted to play I'd have to get in shape, so he had given me a running program and gotten me a job driving a Coca Cola truck for the summer. He said loading and unloading the crates of Coke would get me in shape fast.

The first day on the job with Coca Cola, I was briefed on how to handle customers and how to load and unload the truck.

I also got a firm warning that "if you turn the corner too sharply, all the bottles will fall off one side of the truck and spill onto the street." Broken coke bottles scattered all over a major metropolitan thoroughfare in the traffic, they said, made a mess I wouldn't believe.

In spite of having been warned, I wheeled around a corner one day—and I've never heard a more shattering noise than the sound of all those bottles hitting the street. To make matters worse, the route supervisor was in the truck with me that day. I thought I was through. My heart beat like a triphammer and waves of self-accusation and self-pity rolled over me. As I saw it during those fleeting moments there was no way out of the disaster I had created. But my supervisor was very calm and said quietly, "Just stop the truck, get out, collect the unbroken bottles, sweep up the mess, and don't fret about it." I did, and an hour and a half later the street was clear.

That episode on the Coke truck came to mind as I surveyed our garbage truck dilemma. Yes, I'd made a mistake in our calculations, and, yes, the garbage truck was too small. But I began immediately to survey this new mess and to figure a way to clean it up.

During those moments I remembered, too, that I was committed to go on and build the business *no matter what.* So, although I was scared, I didn't ask, "Shall I go on?" but rather, "Which way shall I go from here to solve this problem?"

The question now was: how could I raise additional capital to purchase a bigger truck? Slowly, a plan emerged—take on another subdivision, prebill them for three months with the agreement that we would start servicing them sixty days later. And that's what we did. We contracted with and prebilled another subdivision—and then a third.

By the time the third subdivision was under control we had raised $25 thousand capital by selling 20 percent of the business to four friends, and we were able to purchase two additional larger trucks. In a few months we were picking up garbage from almost five thousand homes. Most mornings I was either driving or working on a truck, but I still managed to maintain my accounting practice.

After several more months I decided to expand from the residential into the "commercial" garbage collection business. In our area this meant mostly apartment buildings. The day I made the decision to go ahead there was an opportunity to get the business at a high-rise apartment complex, The Houston House. The owners were faced with an immediate and serious problem—there was no one to collect the garbage the day they called. We were working to full capacity in the daytime, but I really wanted that account. When I couldn't get anyone else to go, I got in a truck by myself and worked four hours that night removing garbage from every floor of The Houston House.

My arms and shoulders ached by the time I'd carried all those garbage cans down to the truck and then back up to each apartment. But I kept saying to myself, "So this is what it takes. This is what it takes." I had promised myself I was going to make it no matter *what* it took. And I was finding out what that was.

One morning, while working in a distant part of our subdivision, I was picking up the cans at the back door of one of the homes. A woman in her robe called from her back porch, "Would you mind carrying a couple of extra boxes out for me?" I said I'd be glad to, and did. We were at the end of a street, so I jumped in the cab with the driver. Just as we were pulling out, the woman called to us to wait. She hurried out, pressed a five-dollar bill into my hand and stepped back from the truck. I hesitated, but then smiled and thanked her and put the money up on the dashboard for the driver.

That day a friend of Diane's was playing bridge at the country club. One of the women playing at the same table said, "The saddest thing happened today. There was the nicest looking young man working on our street as a *garbage* man. And as the truck drove off I noticed that he was wearing a *Rice University ring!"* Diane's friend had to struggle to keep from laughing, but she didn't say a thing.

By this time our business was really going well. My dad had come on board full time and was working on the back of trucks when he was needed, as well as keeping the machinery going.

I continued driving a truck for over a year. I wanted to learn the waste business thoroughly, to know how much time it actually took to work a block or make a round trip to the dump. Such information would be invaluable to us if we expanded further.

Some days I'd get up very early, work on a route from four to eight, then take a shower, change into my president-of-the-company-and-accounting-partner clothes and get on with the day. I was working almost all the time, and although I had an incredible amount of energy, I was just barely able to keep my nose above the water in each area of my life.

I have to smile now when I think of my own intensity to get the job done in those days. Within a few weeks after we started we began to experience truck breakdowns. One day the compactor didn't work on the large truck I was driving, and we had about seventy more homes to service before completing the route. When the compactor went out, I was determined to finish the route. I called out to my helpers, "Hey, one of you guys jump in the truck and we'll throw the cans up, and you can stomp the garbage down." Both of them said they weren't about to get into the truck with all that garbage, so I climbed up into the truck. That was when I found myself up to my armpits in garbage.

As I was getting out of the truck that day, I thought to myself, "Life really isn't bad at all." The company was going well, and we were getting new business. A sense of well-being flooded my thoughts.

As we were moving toward the beginning of 1968, the accounting firm was growing rapidly, and American Refuse Systems had overcome its lack of capitalization due to my miscalculations. We had really worked hard. It had been a very intense price to pay, but I loved what I was doing, and things were beginning to look very good.

Then one night as I walked up to our house after a long but satisfying day, Diane burst out the front door, and I could tell by the look on her face that something terrible had happened. "It's your dad," she said. "He's had a bad heart attack."

Chapter 2

A LITTLE LEAGUER IN THE LAND OF GIANTS

I had never seen my father look like that—helpless, and very pale. I was deeply shaken and felt a strange sense of unreality as I stood by his hospital bed. When I started home I thought about how fragile even very important things like life and success really were. I loved my dad, and the thought that he could be brought down so quickly frightened me. Yesterday he had been a strong "he-man" working on heavy equipment and throwing loaded garbage cans around with the best of the younger men. Today, he was helpless. I realized how little there was in life that I could really control.

It was the beginning of a bad time for me. Dad's illness would obviously put a strain on the garbage company operation. But what I didn't count on was that several other problems were going to catch me at the same time, and that the combined pressure would almost plow me under.

I had agreed previously to help a friend start a special kind of financial consulting business. We'd just begun working on the business, and he had hired several very capable employees. Within a few days of my father's heart attack, this friend got very sick also and had to go to the hospital. I tried to help his employees get started working with the clients my friend had contacted, but it was also tax season and *our* accounting firm was at its busiest time ever. And to add to the burden our garbage company had just taken on another large contract, and we were operating with new and inexperienced employees.

Within a week I was almost frantic. My food wouldn't seem to digest, and I had a big knot in my chest. When I was doing one thing, I thought of two others which had to be done that same day.

The pressure just kept building. Even though it was cold, my body was damp from continuous perspiration. Since so much of what I was doing in the accounting firm had to be done by the end of the tax year and involved important decisions with key clients, I needed to spend time thinking through problems and consulting with them as they made decisions. I was caught in a triangle of pressing demands, and I felt my throat constricting as if there were wire around my neck.

During those days my thinking would get fuzzy; I'd feel weak and think I was going to pass out. I began to be afraid that I was losing control, and would break out in a cold sweat when that thought hit me. The pressure became so great that one afternoon I got in my car after lunch and couldn't remember whether I was going to the accounting office or the truck yard. I almost panicked.

That night I was exhausted, but I couldn't sleep. As I stared at the ceiling, I fantasized all our trucks breaking down at the same time. I was trying to push each of them myself in order to get them going. My heart began beating faster in the darkness and my body was chilled. The horrible thought that we might fail almost paralyzed me.

I wanted to quit and run away. I was scared to death, very lonely, and sick of the whole deal. As hard as I tried to think about my life and what was important to me, my mind was just a confused mass of muddled images.

Just then in my imagination I saw a picture of myself sitting under a big oak tree on the Rice University campus, deciding not to take advantage of my last chance to play football. And then I remembered committing myself to make it in the garbage business "whatever it takes!" I lay back on my pillow and felt a deep sigh within myself—"Good Lord, so *this* is what it takes," I thought, then rolled over and got some restless sleep.

Finally, I realized I was about to crack. The only way I could keep going was to ration out the decision-making—to allow myself to make only three high-pressure decisions a day. If

I'd made three by twelve noon, I just wouldn't let myself consider anything of real significance until the next day. I'd work on lesser matters and refuse to think beyond that.

Slowly I began to develop strength, and my physical symptoms subsided. Although things didn't go perfectly in any direction, each of the businesses seemed to make it through those crisis days without major failures. The employees of my friend (with his blessing) went to work for their best client. I had a partner in the accounting business who rescued us by really coming through and performing superbly.

As for the garbage business, we survived—that's about all I can say about that. But I learned some very important things about facing adversity calmly, about trusting other people around me and not thinking the entire world rests on my shoulders.

My dad began to get better, and tax season ended. One day I woke up and smelled the earth after a late spring rain, and I sighed clear to my toes. We had survived. And a month later we entered into a profitable contract with the city of Houston to dispose of part of the residential garbage which was under city collection agreements.

At this time we had built the company to a point at which we had about $300 thousand annual revenue, $120 thousand capital and approximately $80 thousand in the bank. Everything we made was plowed back into expansion.

As a means of improving our position, we had come up with some inexpensive ways to compete with other companies that had more money and could afford the more expensive equipment. For instance, instead of the high metal containers, we built attractive wooden boxes into which a number of smaller barrels could be inserted. Since they looked better, people liked them. And they were much cheaper to install.

In addition, I went to seminars around the country to learn all I could about the solid waste business. And we thought of every possible way we could improve the service to customers over that of our competitors. It was fun figuring out ways to improve service, and I think we really caught our competition off guard.

But our progress was not without setbacks. Just at that time a larger company in a city in the Southern part of the U.S. went bankrupt. They had had an excellent reputation. We were appointed trustee and felt this was our opportunity to move into a major market, to really prove to the entire solid waste industry that we had very good management capabilities. Flexing our muscles, we accepted the appointment. But the end result was that we *lost* several hundreds of thousands of dollars.

By 1968 we had been in business about two years and had almost a million dollars in annual sales. We decided to try to expand into two or three other Texas cities. After doing some checking, we drew up a plan which included the raising of $600 thousand additional capital through a private stock sale.

It just happened that at that time a man named Lou Waters had become head of the corporate finance department of Underwood, Neuhaus in Houston, the company which was handling our private placement. The straightforward way Lou Waters dealt with us and his obvious knowledge of corporate finance really impressed me. After some difficulties, we worked out the placement and got the money.

But before we moved on this expansion plan, I made a three-week trip across America. I wanted to look at the solid waste business and visit with people considered to be the most outstanding operators of garbage companies in key cities in the United States.

When I drove to the Houston International airport to begin that trip, I was an excited twenty-eight-year-old who was enjoying the building of a growing local business. As I began to talk to the best garbage company operators in the world, I was impressed with their dedication to the business of keeping their communities clean. I listened to what they had to say, and was surprised that several of these men began to discuss their problems with me. It seemed that few people had realized the effect the *enormous* increase in solid waste was beginning to have in the cities.

Almost all the companies needed additional capital to expand their services—just to take care of their present clients, not to mention the hundreds of thousands of new residential and commercial customers moving into the cities every week. Not only was the increase in waste material a practical difficulty in itself, but the ecologists also had seen that the burning of garbage was posing serious health problems. Recent governmental regulations had eliminated this major way to dispose of the mammoth mountains of garbage. So existing companies were having to learn the landfill business to survive, and this involved even greater needs for capital.

I moved on across the country. In one city, an older operator talked about the fact that if he died his estate would be crippled because of the high estate taxes his heirs would have to pay. And since a garbage company's assets are very illiquid, the heirs could be wiped out with no source of cash to pay the taxes. By the time my tour was over, I saw that this was a general problem in the industry.

Another serious problem I discovered was that these very capable independent operators were feeling severe competition from a couple of large emerging regional companies with new capital.

One night at the end of the second week I sat down alone in my hotel room and began to jot down some of the things I was discovering. I'd come on this trip to learn how to be a better operator, because we were about to expand into two additional cities. But something very different was happening to me. I was beginning to see a need and an opportunity which was so large, so preposterous, that my mind wouldn't consider it at first.

Since I had come to learn, I had been listening and asking questions of some very successful and capable men—presidents of outstanding businesses. For some reason—perhaps because no one had ever come to listen, perhaps because the pressures had built inside with no one to tell them to—these men had also told me about their personal needs and frustrations relating to the industry as a whole.

As I sat there in my room in the Radisson Hotel, looking out the window at the streets of Minneapolis, I saw pieces of paper swirling in the wind down the almost-slick black street.

And I realized that, at that moment in history, I might be one of the few people anywhere to see the nature of the crisis America was facing. The difficulties behind the scenes in the garbage industry, combined with the problems of disposing of the garbage itself, could become horrendous if something didn't change.

It dawned on me then that I was beginning to see an emerging need for a large *national* solid-waste company in America, a company which could provide the capital and know-how to coordinate residential and commercial collection and disposal operations, including subsidiary services like landfills and equipment design and manufacture. The stock of a large national company could be used to purchase existing companies; this would give the present owners better liquidity. The larger company could provide the capital to take advantage of the new opportunities in the industry. And it would provide the independent companies a chance to be on a team of superior operators who could take care of any regional bullies who threatened to wipe them out in the present near-crisis situation.

It may sound corny, but I was awed at the opportunity, and the sense of being at the "right place at the right time" which I was experiencing. It was as if, through a "voice in the night," God was telling me, "The time to build this national company is right now, Tom, and you're the man who's supposed to do it!"

I had chill bumps all over my arms and back. I shook my head and laughed out loud. "You're crazy, Fatjo," I said to the empty room. "With two years' experience in a little home-owned company you're going to buy out the major operators in the world! Sure!" But in my imagination I could already see our blue trucks in the early morning fog moving out into empty streets and alleys all over America. I imagined myself negotiating purchase contracts with the owners of companies we would be acquiring. The owners seemed proud to be part of the largest and best company of its kind in the world. Suddenly I realized I was envisioning a company with hundreds of millions of dollars a year in sales. It was ridiculous, and yet somehow I knew it could be done!

Chapter 3

THE FASTEST ROLLER COASTER IN TEXAS

When I got home, I had a whole new goal for our company—to become the largest and best solid waste company in the world! That was my dream.

I liked what I'd seen of the people I had met in the industry. They were tough, strong, and independent, right out of a Charles Bronson or Clint Eastwood movie, with a touch of John Wayne. They believed in what they were doing, worked hard, played hard, and didn't take anything off anybody. I liked the idea of being on a team with them.

By the time I stepped off the plane in Houston, I had already begun to design a plan for building a national corporation by acquiring the best operating company in each of the major cities of America. I decided not to share my idea with anyone until I had pretty well worked out the details of the plan for making the acquisitions. I knew that my colleagues in our company would think I was insane if I didn't have the figures on paper. But as the plan unfolded, I saw that it would work and felt we could do it.

When I finally unveiled my dream, my associates may have thought I was crazy, but there were the facts and a solid plan to put a national company together. So they almost had to go along with me. Besides, I seemed to have enough enthusiasm for us all. I *knew* we'd stumbled onto an important idea which had come of age. And so, under my leadership, a flea-sized company seemed to be setting out to capture a herd of live elephants. At least, as I look back, I can see it must have seemed that way.

For twelve months we traveled across the country attempting to make acquisitions. People were interested, but we had absolutely *no* success in consummating a single purchase.

I couldn't believe it. I'd been *sure* I was right about a national company being the best solution for the operators we were talking to. At first I felt myself sinking into my old fear of not ever really being able to make it all the way to the top. But I'd learned through the Coke bottle accident and the hard times I'd just weathered that there are ways I'd never thought of to recover from adversity—if I'd just keep looking. So we talked over what we might do, and, after we'd brainstormed every approach we could think of, I called Lou Waters at Underwood, Neuhaus, who had helped us out before.

The next afternoon, when I had outlined our approach to acquiring companies and described our total failure, I asked Lou what he thought was wrong. After thinking about it for a few minutes, he said, "I see basically three difficulties: one's the lack of proper organization, another's your lack of financial credibility and negotiability for your stock, and third, there's the lack of really large company management experience."

I sat there looking at Lou. I knew I had the energy, the desire, the development capability, and an adequate knowledge of the industry to build a sound company. But I saw clearly that I lacked experience and judgment in large financial moves and changes. In fact, in the league we were trying to get into, I just didn't know how to "think big" financially. I realized then that the ingredients Lou had pointed to were essential to the building of a national company, and I simply didn't have them.

After spending the afternoon with Lou, I saw that, for an undertaking as large as the one I envisioned, we needed to have someone with these financial abilities leading us.

And Lou Waters was the logical choice. But with his experience and stature there was no place for him in our organization except at the very top. It seemed strange to ask someone to come in at that level, and I had an uneasy feeling about giving up the number-one position in my own company. But I remembered that my goal was to build the largest and best company of its kind in the world. And I knew we really needed Lou's experience to accomplish that.

So, after several months of negotiations, we finally convinced him to be the Chairman of the company. Lou's experience in the areas of acquisition and finance immediately helped us solve the first problem he had pinpointed.

Our problem of financial credibility stemmed partly from the fact that our own company stock, with which we had tried to purchase other companies, was privately held. This did not provide the liquidity the owners were looking for. What we needed was a publicly held company with a solid reputation.

Timing was again in our corner. Browning-Ferris Machinery Company was an old, conservatively run machinery company which had maintained a level of sales of about $15 million for the previous ten years and had earned approximately $800 thousand before taxes each year during that period. The company had $4½ million in equity, no debt, and had made a small public offering back in the mid-1950s. And, just as we were looking, the controlling interest in that company became available, so we made our move.

With the acquisition of Browning-Ferris, we gained a name, public identity, and credibility into which we could merge American Refuse Systems. I was awed at the way things seemed to be waiting to happen as we moved ahead. And I kept remembering how much I had wanted to quit and run when things weren't going well.

With the merger we changed our name to Browning-Ferris Industries. And in October 1969 we moved out on the acquisition trail again.

In November of 1969 we acquired our first company in Cincinnati for a combination of cash and BFI stock. But from then on we stayed with stock transactions, using first preferred and then, gradually, common stocks with the use of an "earn out."* In February 1970 we acquired a company in Bridge City, Texas.

---

* The "earn out" is an opportunity for the stockholder to receive more stock based on increased performance from a profitability point of view.

And then—almost overnight, it seemed—we acquired companies in Cleveland, Ohio; Baltimore, Maryland; Detroit, Michigan; and Minneapolis, Minnesota.

As our momentum picked up, we saw that the companies we were acquiring had varying styles of internal management and different levels of management expertise and efficiency. We realized that, to bring the emerging national company's overall efficiency and productivity up to a very high level, we were going to need someone with a great deal of quality experience in large waste company operations—experience I didn't have—as operating head of BFI.

My search brought me to a man named Harry Phillips who had successful operations in Houston, Memphis, and San Juan, Puerto Rico. After some thought I realized Harry was the man who could integrate the various companies we were acquiring. His respect in the industry was unquestioned, and he was the kind of man people could work with on the tough, practical problems of implementing a merger.

So here again I was faced with an unusual decision. The only place for Harry Phillips on the team was in the top operating manager's position.

I had to take a long hard look at what I wanted and ask myself what my goal at this point really was. And when I realized again that the goal I was clearly committed to was to build the largest and best solid waste company in the world, the choice was clear. After some serious negotiations, we were able to convince Harry Phillips to join BFI as president of the company.

At that point, BFI moved ahead dramatically in terms of new acquisitions, operational efficiency, coordination of all efforts, and success in the market place.

In this age of bigness it may not be easy to grasp the magnitude of what I had in mind, given the facts of who we were and what we had. We were one small new company in an industry with hundreds of large, well-established single and multicity operations. I was proposing that we buy the best company in every city of any size in America and integrate them all into one smoothly functioning company, and I proposed that we make all these acquisitions more or less at the same time.

Since that was my goal I realized that I'd have to have a plan which would leave nothing undone. And I developed what I was later to call an action plan. I listed every step and skill that would be required to acquire a company. Then we took each step and broke it down into all the necessary functions and people to make it happen. When we finished we had a plan which we felt could handle the acquisition and integration of any number of companies.

We developed a kind of assembly-line model for acquiring companies to make sure every necessary task was planned in detail—from the initial contact to the final integration and successful operation of the acquired company under the BFI banner. For this growth-by-acquisition period, we divided the company into three distinct areas of responsibility: development, administration and management. A different person was made responsible for each of the three areas. Lou Waters was responsible for administration, Harry Phillips for management, and I was responsible for development. Each of us ran our section as though it were an entire company under our responsibility.*

As we began to acquire companies, the individuals reporting to us had similar, almost autonomously handled responsibilities. To give you an idea of the depth of management experience we finally had, almost all of our negotiators had previously been senior officers in other companies and/or were very experienced in their operations.

Lou, Harry, and I met with our new team and refined our action plans, checking the feasibility of each step as far as we could. Then we committed ourselves to the plan and to

---

* Within the *development* segment there were four distinct areas: acquisitions, market development, sales, and corporate affairs. Within the *administration* segment there were three areas: finance, accounting, and legal management. *Management* involved all operating personnel. Certain staff capabilities such as engineering and insurance were also included in the management area.

our parts of the "assembly line," and turned back to the big push to acquire and assimilate the best companies available.

What happened then was to me like a fun-starved ghetto kid getting into Disneyland for the first time. We really had a good time, even though we worked many twenty-two-hour days.

Each member of each group knew his or her responsibilities. Everyone knew when to go into action. For example, in the acquisition effort, one team member would introduce Browning-Ferris to a prospective company by making an evaluation presentation to the acquisition team.

If we approved of going ahead, a negotiator would first visit the company and make a judgment relating to the management capability of the owner. Immediately, there would be an operating review; then we would bring the owner to Houston so that he could develop a better understanding of Browning-Ferris's objectives, and so that we could better judge his probable compatibility with our team and with our approach to the solid waste industry. During that visit, he would meet key members of the management team, and we would try to understand his goals and basic approach to doing business. Then, if all was satisfactory, we would make an offer.

Further negotiations would usually take place, and finally we would reach an agreement. Immediately, the legal department would start to draw up the documents, and the accounting section would begin the integration process. From then on it was up to the management section to make all operating decisions and to make sure the new company was melding into our bunch as smoothly as possible. Watching each section move into action as the deal reached that group's responsibility point was beautiful to see.

During the next twenty-four months, we acquired over one hundred companies.

Chapter 4

WINNING, BUT GETTING TOO INVOLVED IN THE GARBAGE

The atmosphere at the company during those years was like that surrounding a winning professional football team. We were working very hard, and everything we did seemed to succeed. I could hardly believe what was happening. People started wanting to become a part of our team. And we tried to make the kinds of trades which would allow the owners of the companies we bought to do much better than they could have done on their own.

In every area of our business I found myself in a new world. For example, our first credit line at the Republic National Bank in Dallas, right after we took over Browning-Ferris in 1969, was for a million dollars, and that was very hard to come by. By late 1971, our credit line was over $160 million.

I had decided that I would go anywhere at any time to complete an acquisition. And I personally participated in more than one hundred fifty types of completed negotiations for BFI from 1969 to 1973. I had enormous amounts of desire and enthusiasm—all totally focused on what we were doing. And I really believed that we were a part of an idea that was totally right for the companies we were acquiring, for BFI, and for America. So I simply went to these company owners and laid all my cards on the table. There was no need to be sly. We had a good deal for them which would meet many of their basic personal and corporate needs. We wanted them in the cause and on the team with us. And they came with us. Dozens of companies were in the process of joining us at the same time.

We were very sincere about building a team and placing the emphasis on people as we built BFI. I developed a real love for the people whose companies we were acquiring. I was deeply dedicated to being loyal to them and their interests and was determined that we just weren't going to let them down. The relationships with some of those company owners and their families became very important to me. With all its speed and size, the company was developing in a very personal way.

This was a very heady life for an insecure twenty-nine-year-old who had been programmed all his life to some day "be a man." Things were going well, and I was beginning to get some real confidence in the power available to get things done through planning with a creative team of people.

What was happening to me as a person was that I became a garbage man through and through. I had always repressed many of my basic feelings behind a calm façade of conservatism. But as I began to identify with these strong people, many of whom were hard-working, heavy-drinking men (and of course many were not), I joined the free-living bunch.

In the atmosphere of acquiring five companies per month for over two years, I had only one goal: to build BFI. All other normal life was put in abeyance. I would work hard all day long—all night long if necessary. And I was often in four or five cities in one week. Typically, after a long hard day, we'd start drinking before dinner, continue through dinner, and then stay out at the bars until the wee hours of the morning. I found I had a violent side to my nature; I was ready to fight after a few drinks.

Those weeks and months became a blur. I remember one night in Atlanta. I had so much to drink that I could hardly move when I got back to my hotel at dawn, but I took a shower and made an important breakfast meeting. When I reached for my water glass, my hand was shaking so much that I knew I couldn't risk eating or drinking anything for fear of embarrassing myself.

Once when closing a deal I stayed up for forty-eight hours with no sleep, working in the daytime and playing at night. The second night I remember becoming aware that I was barefoot, wading in a creek in the woods with my suit on. I turned out to be about thirty or forty miles out of the city. I drove back to the hotel, changed clothes, and somehow was at the company's office early to work on the deal.

Now I realize I was fortunate that I made it through those years without serious injury or without blowing an important deal. But at the time I felt like a character out of one of Harold Robbins's books—someone who could make no mistakes. Many of our negotiations were melodramatic. I remember once we were about to close a deal with an important company in Baltimore. We were sitting in a restaurant with the owner of the company when the representatives from another large company came in and offered to take him in a Lear jet on a tour of their company. The man we were dealing with looked a little embarrassed, but we told him to go ahead and look, that we'd be right there when he got back.

In the course of the trip our rivals offered the Baltimore owner a million dollars more than we had (in that company's stock). But he decided to bet on us. We didn't have a plane in those days, but after the deal was closed we rented a Lear jet and took the owner and his wife to the industry's national convention in San Francisco. We were telling them in loud clear language that we were going to follow through with the kind of loyalty and good intentions we stressed throughout our negotiations.

All this was taking place so fast I didn't have time to even consider what might be happening to me as a person. Looking back, some things are like a strange dream. My family had become like shadows in the background and seemed very distant. We had a second child by this time, a boy we named Tom. I loved my kids but really didn't give them much time.

Later, I was going to realize just how much my lifestyle needed changing. But at the time I just charged on. I had cut loose from the strictness of my childhood and felt like I imagined a man would feel who was succeeding in getting things done in a very tough world.

This was a strange time. We were winning in the biggest game in the world—American business—and winning at a speed that was almost unbelievable. By 1973 we had gone from one million dollars in sales to about $300 million in three years. We had gone from operating in one location to operating in hundreds (centered in one hundred thirty cities). Our stock was selling at fifty to sixty times earnings.

But 1973 was also the year Diane and I were divorced. I feel a great sadness as I realize how little I understood about living and relating at that time. In the next few years I was to have to take a hard look at my personal life and my private finances—which I'll talk about later.

At the time, though, my mind was centered almost totally on BFI. By 1973 most of the acquisitions were completed; we had built the largest solid-waste company in the world. The next step was to make sure it was developed into the best.

As a part of the action planning for the new corporate management phase of the company's life, we initiated a system of regional vice presidents. Our plan was to gather from each of our new companies the best operational methods, equipment designs, and sales approaches.

After working the bugs out of the resulting procedures, we developed a controllable consistency of policies. We saw a regularity and orderliness develop within the whole company in a very short time.

Up to this point Harry Phillips, Lou Waters, and I had been coexecutive officers. After three years of the transition period into the operational phase of management, I resigned as an officer, although I stayed active as a board member. I felt I had made the contribution to BFI I'd set out to make, and I wanted to try my hand at building and acquiring other companies not related to the solid waste business. After another two years, Harry Phillips became the sole chief executive officer, with Lou Waters continuing as chairman of the board. And with these management changes, most of the transition from the acquisition building team to the operational management team was virtually completed. From 1973 to 1980, the management team and the new plans took the annual sales to $552 million.*

We had won! We had built the largest and best solid waste company in the world. But what did it all mean?

* * *

I backed off from all the activity and began to think back over the breathless few years I'd just been through. I knew I'd stumbled onto a way to get things done in a very materialistic world. But where was I going with what I'd learned?

One day while driving through an old neighborhood in Richmond, Texas, thinking about what had happened in my life, I passed the grade school and pulled up and stopped on an impulse. As I got out, I reached back and got my jacket; there was a fall chill in the air. I was walking across the playing field when I stopped. Something was very familiar. Then I remembered. One time years before, when I'd been nine years old, I had tackled the big kid from down the street—what was his name?—and almost knocked him out. It seemed like a hundred years ago.

Then I'd been so scared and yet so proud and ambitious in my efforts to show my dad I could make it and "be a man." And I realized now that I'd helped build a business empire to prove something about that to the world—or to myself. I smiled. There were a couple of things I'd learned for sure, and one was that being a real man is something very different from building a big company. And I had learned some things about accomplishing goals in spite of being afraid to fail, things which I felt could help anyone succeed in reaching his or her dreams. And those things I wanted to share somehow.

---

* As we were in our rapid expansion period, we acquired a company which was in the secondary fiber waste paper business. We took the sales of that company from $18 million to $180 million, but then spun it off prior to 1980. It operates now as a separate company called Consolidated Fibres, Inc., and is sold over the counter. Its sales were considered part of BFI's in 1973 but not in 1980.

PART TWO

The Art of Creative Enterprise—A Process

Introduction

THE PROCESS OF CREATIVE BUILDING

During the years from 1966–76, when I was involved with the building of Browning-Ferris Industries, we were moving so fast, dealing with such quantities of information and money and so many new people that we had very little time to reflect on *how* we were accomplishing our seemingly impossible goals.

At the time I figured our success was due to all the talented executives we'd gotten on our team. But after I left an active management role with BFI I was involved in the development of several other corporations. In one instance, as I set out to build a company called The Houstonian, I was afraid, because this time I was building a company alone. It was when I was dreaming about that project that I began consciously to isolate the attitudes, principles, and procedures which had helped me accomplish my goals for BFI.

I came to see that these attitudes and procedures, if considered properly, can virtually guarantee the successful outcome of a business venture or other vocational goal—as well as many personal goals. Put together, they form what I call the process of creative enterprise.

My friend, Keith Miller, after trying this process in his own life for twelve months, has encouraged me to share the following with you. Together we have written the description of what we think it takes to find and accomplish large goals such as the building of a successful business or an individual vocation.

Although we are continuing to use the first person singular in my name, some of the insights and ideas are Keith's.

When we speak of the "creative enterprise process," we will not just be describing a series of mechanical "steps to take." Rather, we will be talking more about attitudes, human drives, and principles for selecting and translating certain dreams into realities.

Of course, careful organization and planning are essential to success, and we'll take a hard look at these. But we will also be spending a good deal of time discussing various aspects of emotion—desire, fear, egotism, pride. It is true that when it comes to building large businesses, such factors may seem marginal to the problems of capitalization, management designs, and corporate game plans, which we'll also discuss. But as crucial as these subjects are, I am now convinced that emotion and the handling of ego drives are the keys to the success of any venture.

It is important to recognize that the creative enterprise process we will be describing is not for every goal in life, but only for those major goals: starting out after college to fulfill the dreams of one's life, changing vocations in midstream, revitalizing a department in a major company, building a new business, or perhaps beginning a new profession after having been a homemaker for years or having retired. We hope this section will help provide a practical frame in which your own vocational dream can be captured and realized.

Some of the elements of successful achievement we discuss here have to do with the creation of large corporate ventures, and others pertain only to accomplishing individual vocational dreams. But it is our feeling that the principles underlying the following chapters could also be used to transform very large social, political, and religious institutions.

Because of what's happening to us we hope the process we describe can open new doorways toward the fulfillment of your dreams.

Chapter 5

DESIRE

Intense personal desire is a quality which is absolutely essential to succeeding with the process of creative enterprise. I hope all kinds of people will read and enjoy these pages, but I confess that I am writing primarily to a certain kind of person—one who wants very much to risk going after his or her dreams but has always been afraid to. I am writing to you who would love to enjoy the thrill of the struggle to achieve . . . who would like to put yourselves in the ring . . . who have an intense desire to become more than you are. I believe that men and women with this kind of intense drive are the ones who get things done. When an idea captures their imaginations, they move themselves and their ventures through the inevitable setbacks to the completion of their dreams.

I played high school football against a fellow named Fred Hansen, and then we both went on to attend Rice University in Houston. Fred was a natural athlete and developed into a star pole vaulter. In 1964 he participated in the Tokyo Olympics and worked his way right up to the finals. The struggle for the winning spot went on for several hours. The pressure became almost unbearable, even to the spectators. But with incredible desire and intense concentration Fred kept coming, again and again. And his raw determination and courage finally paid off when he overcame all opposition and was awarded the first-place gold medal.

Did he win because of natural athletic ability? Obviously,

that was important, but I will always believe that in addition to his disciplined training and highly tuned physical endurance, he kept focused and achieved his goal because of tremendous desire and singleness of purpose.

Fred wanted to be the best pole vaulter in the world. And he wanted it more than anything else. Now, he has gone on to become a successful dentist in Houston. While he probably hasn't pole vaulted for years, his desire for personal excellence has become a way of life for him and is now expressed in new and different ways. For instance, several years ago Fred took up golf as a hobby. He worked persistently to perfect his game and is now a sub-par golfer.

Obviously, very few of us are going to win Olympic gold medals or become sub-par golfers, but I am convinced that there is secret desire in most of us to commit ourselves to an interest or a cause. And when it becomes focused on a specific goal, it is this secret desire to achieve which is a key to succeeding in *any* creative enterprise.

No one seems to know where this kind of desire comes from, but I believe that as a person becomes aware of it and its life-changing possibilities, it can be disciplined and channeled into a rewarding lifestyle. I discovered, in my experience in the garbage business and in subsequent ventures, that this same kind of desire can be uncovered, brought into focus and nurtured in other people. If you, in reading these pages, feel an inner stirring to change and to do something different that might fulfill a lifelong dream, I hope you will open the door to that possibility, because that act of *really opening yourself* to changing your life (and believing it's possible) can release a heightened sense of desire. And that desire can provide the motivational energy to begin making the change.

As I was describing my own beginnings in business earlier, I became aware of how inadequate words are to express the intense desire I felt to succeed. The decision to pay any price that was moral or legal to reach my goals in building a company was overwhelming for me personally. Obviously the expression of this desire will vary according to a person's emotional background and life situation. For example, some people might think working a twelve- to sixteen-hour day or working on Saturdays would reflect an intense desire, while others would consider that it would take a seven-day, sixteen-hours-a-day, all-consuming schedule to express an intense desire. Other people don't think of time worked at all but of emotional focus. They might put all their thoughts and energies into being a "super mother" or "super father" or the best child in the family. But each person who has it will express this desire in some continuous kinds of behaviors toward a certain end. To me it meant that I would identify and overcome every specific problem I encountered in building and managing the company.

Through this attitude I began to realize there is almost always a solution to every problem out there somewhere if the desire to succeed is strong enough. I am, of course, aware that there may be devastating changes or new inventions which can wipe out a whole way of life or an industry. For example, the flexibility and speed of automobile, truck, and air transportation have now left the railroads high and dry. But, apart from these kinds of situations, I believe more problems can be solved because of desire and tenacity than most people would believe.

I recall one time during a closing of an $80 million public stock offering in New York that we received word from the newly organized Price Commission that BFI might have violated price guidelines. Consequently, our attorneys would not let us close the offering, which was going to provide a tremendous amount of capital for our company and shareholders.

We spent the next four days in the office of Manny Cohen at Wilmer, Cutler & Pickering in Washington. We concentrated day and night on the problem, literally sleeping in the reception room until we worked our way through to a proper and reasonable solution. Then we were able to move ahead and close the public offering. The exhilaration of getting through this sort of difficulty not only brings new enthusiasm and confidence, but it also rekindles the strength of the original desire.

It may seem that I am placing excessive emphasis on the importance of the kind of desire we've been describing here. But I believe that it is absolutely essential to develop the momentum necessary to get through the inevitable difficulties which could otherwise overwhelm one in the establishing and building of new business ventures, other vocations, and avocations.

And besides being a help with meeting adversity, this kind of desire can help overcome some of the most inhibiting personal hindrances like false pride—which is perhaps the most damaging and blinding characteristic of the would-be creative builder. For instance, I hate to be considered a fool, and I am sensitive to the criticism of people I respect. But when I first decided to build a company "no matter what," I found myself willing to do some strange things, a few of which I've mentioned—like riding inside a garbage truck to finish a route or staying up all night alone to personally collect all the garbage from a large apartment house. I'm sure my friends and associates in the financial world in Houston must have thought I'd lost my mind when I did these things. But somehow, because of my intense desire to build a company, I didn't care.

One component of the kind of desire I'm describing is that one *starts caring more about reaching his or her goals than about the opinions of the people in his or her social world.* And it's hard to estimate how much creative power can be added by that change.

As a matter of fact, this fear of what certain people will think of us may be one of the most crucial factors in the failure of business ventures, political careers, religious institutions, the lives of aspiring writers and artists, and even marriages. People bound by this fear don't seem to be able to capture the imaginations of others sufficiently to initiate creative change.

One of the most profound discoveries I have made, though, is that this kind of desire is contagious. It somehow touches people's imaginations at a deep level and sweeps them along with the instigator or entrepreneur into directions they hadn't planned to go. The desire of the leader evidently offers a "sense of security" for his or her associates. And this atmosphere of security can help them overcome the fear of failure.

I don't pretend to understand why strong positive desire works this way, but it seems to be true that if desire exists in a leader to an intense enough degree, everyone around that leader develops a powerful expectation that a way to success will be found. And I am beginning to believe that this joint expectation has a lot to do with the success which is ultimately achieved in an effort toward any goal.

Can Desire Be Developed?

If intense desire is a necessary component in the creative venturing process, then the big question is: Can it be developed?

I believe that every normal person has the capacity for the "desire to do well and succeed." But of course this desire is more present in some adults than in others. And its sources probably go back as far as childhood.

Some children are encouraged to believe that they can achieve certain specific things in life—like becoming a champion gymnast or a famous scientist. As a parent attempts to plant such goals in a child's mind, he or she is merely trying to encourage the child to try hard, to exert special effort. But, unfortunately, the child sometimes *receives* this encouragement unconsicously as simply a command to be *fantastic*, be *perfect!* If this happens, the child is likely to feel that he or she will only receive and feel the parent's love and acceptance by excelling. Although the whole transaction may be unconscious to both parent and child, this type of encouragement may be one source of desire.

Some children are raised in poverty or social conditions they view as unacceptable. In such circumstances a child may brood over the situation and make up his or her mind to show the parents or the world that he or she has value. I do not know how much their backgrounds contribute to the focused desire of people as different as actor Anthony Hopkins and football player Jim Plunkett, both of whom came from materially poor families. But both evidence intense desire.

A similar effect can be produced in a child whose parents reject him or her.

Still other children appear to have relatively normal childhoods. But they are encouraged to be a real "man" or a real "woman." This sort of child may grow up looking for some specific way to prove that he or she is in fact a "man" or a "woman." And a desire is born to find some way to make the proof a matter of public record.

Other children just seem to be born or raised in such a way that they have a large degree of curosity and drive and a great desire for greatness and success.

But whatever the source of the original "desire," I don't believe it will develop unless there are some successes and affirmations along the way which encourage the desire to be expressed. Many people in each of these groups have run into failure and rejection at an early age and have repressed their intense desire as being too dangerous. It is possible, though, for them to have their repressed desire reactivated later by going through some kind of tragedy or failure and realizing that they now have "nothing to lose." At such times they may become open to a cause or a venture or a person who can draw out and cultivate the desire necessary to succeed. There are countless stories of people who report peak experiences, religious conversions, or the awakening of a deep social consciousness following tragedy or failure. Evidently such times can be conducive to becoming reenergized with enormous desire for new life and new creative venturing.

One doesn't know in what ways Simone Weil's trip from Auschwitz concentration camp as one of the few survivors to the presidency of the European Parliament was affected by the shock she endured. But her desire for social change is unquestioned.

It seems to me that the most effective way for intense desire to be developed in a group is for one of the leaders to have and model such desire in his or her own life. Desire then can sometimes be "caught," as it were, from the experiences and attitudes of someone else.

And I am now convinced that, given the right motivation, many more people than I would have expected can uncover within themselves an intense experience of this form of desire.

People in any field who have the desire to succeed remind me in some ways of horses born to race. Someone may have to lead a fine racehorse to the track, but when he gets there, no one has to urge him to run. Similarly, when people with desire finally get unlocked to the opportunity to build a new way of life, a business, or a vocation, their desire seems to burst forth from nowhere. They appear to have the highly focused energy of a fine thoroughbred, often amazing the people around them who never would have expected they were waiting to come out and race toward their dreams.

Chapter 6

CREATIVE DREAMING

Consciously dreaming about the future has evidently been a favorite and uniquely human pastime since the beginning of history. All my life I have enjoyed simply sitting with my feet propped up and fantasizing about the days and years to come. And I still cherish the moments when I can get by myself and daydream to my heart's content.

This kind of conscious dreaming is not the sort of fantasizing that takes place after a person identifies a specific goal, when he or she imagines and pictures the steps necessary for that goal to become a reality. I'm talking about plain and simple daydreaming—just letting one's mind wander where it wants and following it leisurely. At such times I can visualize a variety of directions for my life.

This kind of dreaming doesn't cost anything or hurt anyone. It can bring a lot of happiness. For one thing, it's a shortcut to achieving success, even though it may last for just a few moments and is only in the mind. But in addition, I firmly believe that the seemingly childish practice of daydreaming is a crucial part of the creative enterprise process!

Dreams Can Change the Future

Many people in our culture are taught from childhood that any sort of daydreaming is a waste of time. They see it as a useless pastime that robs us of the time and energy that might better be spent "taking care of our responsibilities." But I believe that is a shortsighted, self-defeating attitude. It is, in my judgment, vitally important for each of us to regularly set aside specific times just to dream—and this is especially true for the entrepreneur-type business person.

Norman Vincent Peale has titled a chapter in one of his books, "The Inflow of New Thoughts Will Remake You." In this chapter he talks about the dreaming process as a powerful inspiration for future development and accomplishment. I agree. In my experience I have found that dreaming will not only change the dreamer, but it can also extend one's real horizons beyond anything that could have been imagined. And at the same time dreaming can open up new and unexpected options which can widen our choices as we look into the future.

There is a paradox involved in this sort of dreaming, though, which keeps some people from taking it seriously. Often the clearest "dream pictures"—the strongest motivators—are simple and almost childlike. For instance, in the beginning stages of developing our first garbage company in Houston, I used to imagine trucks, a whole fleet of blue trucks, rumbling out of our lot onto the streets of Houston in the early morning mist. In my imagination I could "see" the trucks and the men as they wound their way around the streets of our town.

These times of dreaming were not spent engaged in the planning process, figuring out *how* to implement these fantasies. Rather, in my imagination I held dream-pictures of the goals being *already accomplished*. The energy and power those dreams released into my life is absolutely indescribable, particularly later as step-by-step I could see those dreams becoming reality.

Growth Means New Dreams

As the business grew, my dreams changed. In addition to picturing our trucks on the streets of Houston, I began to see myself in the act of signing contracts with subdivisions and successfully negotiating new commercial accounts. Later I dreamed of providing disposal service for the entire city of Houston—the fifth largest city in the country.

And then, as time passed, I began to dream about a national company. This time I could "see" our trucks driving through the streets in cities all across the country. I could "see" the smiles on the faces of owners of other companies as they joined forces with us and became a part of our organization. And later, when these things were starting to happen, the fact that parts of the dream were coming true became a powerful reinforcement of the idea that we could accomplish the entire dream.

Part of the power of creative dreams is that they provide a series of pictures to keep before the mind's eye. They might be compared to the illustrated travel brochures we take with us on a cross-country car trip. The pictures and the copy description change as we move along from one state to another, but they help us get to our destinations. And when a leader has these dream images firmly in mind, other people on the same adventure are reassured by a sense that someone knows where they are going—even though only the leader may actually "see the pictures."

A top executive of Browning-Ferris once apologized to me for an article that had appeared in *Barrons.* He said he was quoted as referring to me as someone who "thought in the future," and he was concerned that I might think the comment was somewhat derogatory. But I told him I was proud just to be mentioned, and then I found myself telling him, "Show me somebody that doesn't dream about the future, and I'll show you a person that doesn't know where he's going." I firmly believe that whenever any business or vocational venture finally becomes successful it is very likely that the end result will be for someone "a dream come true."

Learning How to Dream

So if you have become restless or bored and feel an itch to do new things, to develop new patterns for living—possibly even a new vocational venture, I believe you should unashamedly set aside private time for creative dreaming. Try to imagine yourself doing something different that would really be satisfying or fun.

The best way I've found to dream is to walk by myself on the beach and look out over the Gulf of Mexico. At first my eyes and my mind concentrate only on the water. Gradually the waves and the sky seem to fade away and although my eyes are still open, I am somehow in my imagination. Then I consciously disengage my mind from current problems and let my thoughts drift toward the future. If fantasies of tragedy or failure come, I dismiss them by saying to myself, "It's not time for that kind of thinking. I'm imagining what would be fun to do with my life." I also shut out any negative thoughts about the dreams not being possible for me to accomplish. I have found that some people sabotage their dreams *as they are being born* by looking for reasons the dreams wouldn't work out.

I am aware that all kinds of very personal and disconcerting fantasies can come along to interrupt this process. But when I am engaged in this kind of creative dreaming, I simply tell myself, "I'll deal with that later." Then, in my imagination, I roam on out into the future. Before long I see in my mind's eye some interesting activity—a business deal or a vocational possibility.

At times when you are involved in creative dreaming, you may find that you "sit through" many pictures in your mind before one grabs your imagination with the power to move you to immediate action. But it's important to remember that not every dream is meant for you to act on. Hold out for the picture that excites you, fills you with energy and the desire to get up and do something about it right then. Sometimes when this happens to me I feel as if the dream has selected me! I can see all kinds of exciting ways I would enjoy trying to make the dream happen. I can feel the joy of reaching the goal as I see it happening in my imagination. And my mind is *alive* with ideas and enthusiasm about following up and "doing the dream" as I envision it. Almost before I know it, I am aware that I am already in the process of pursuing the dream to see if it is feasible. And this takes place without my being able to point to a moment when I made a choice. I've just been carried along by the exciting prospect of the dream.

The "Dream" as a Seed

The seed may be an excellent analogy for the creative dream. When most of us see a seed, we can easily mistake it for a small rock or piece of dirt. But the gardener who knows about seeds realizes that within that small and very ordinary looking nondescript particle is a living plant, perhaps even an enormous tree. Even though I know it is true, I still find it hard to accept the truth that within an acorn is the complete engineering design for a giant oak tree.

And I suspect that is an analogy that applies to our real-life dreams, and it certainly carries over into our vocational activities. You may find, after watering and nurturing a particular "seed" you've chosen, that it contains a larger or smaller plant than you thought. But the creative dreamer is one who comes to recognize the "seeds" which look and feel right and nurtures them in dreaming until they begin to grow in the "real world."

This almost mysterious selection of the "right dream" for any given person is, I believe, an intuitive process which happens to different people in different ways. I don't feel it is an art that can be taught; it may well be a gift from God.

I don't know how early an awareness of what dream is right develops in different people. But I read the following story in the *Dallas Morning News* during the summer of 1980 about a young boy who typifies to me the power of creative dreaming.

Astronaut Applauds U.S. Ideals*

Cambridge, Mass. (AP)—Franklin Chang left home with a dream: to become an astronaut.

When the 18-year-old got off a plane from Costa Rica 12

* This article appeared June 13, 1980, and is used by permission of The Associated Press.

years ago, he had $50 in his pocket and spoke only Spanish. But he had his dream.

Today, at age 30, Dr. Franklin Chang is a nuclear physicist and an American citizen. Only July 7, he starts training to fly on the space shuttle, one of 19 men and women chosen in the latest group of astronauts.

Chang, grandson of a Chinese emigrant, son of a Costa Rican service station owner, said the secret of his success is simple. He owes it, he said, to the traditional American ideals: ambition and tenacity and hard work—attributes his folks told him make people prosper and get ahead in the United States.

"You have a dream, and if you really work at it, you can make it happen," he said.

Ever since he was a little boy, Chang wanted to be a spaceman. As best he can remember, the dream began in 1957, the day the Soviets launched Sputnik I and the space age began.

"When I was 7 years old, my mother told me one day that the Russians had put up an artificial satellite around the Earth, and if I went out in the yard in the evening and climbed up a tree, I could see it go by," he said. "Well, I went out and climbed a tree, but I didn't see anything. But I remember that vividly."

Chang became a space fan. He kept a scrapbook of the American and Russian space feats. He knew the names of all the rockets and capsules and astronauts.

"My high school classmates were into it as well," he said. "We had little teams of space cadets who were going to go into space. Slowly, my friends began to get interested in other things, and by the time I graduated from high school, I was the only one who still wanted to be an astronaut. I was the only one who hadn't grown up yet."

So he went seeking his dream. His father bought him a plane ticket to Hartford, Conn., where he lived with distant relatives and repeated his senior year in high school. He stayed with them for four months, then boarded with other local families.

Teacher Allan Winter took it upon himself to teach Chang English. He started the teen-ager on Bertrand Russell's History of Western Civilization.

"That was my first book in English," he said. "It took me about a year, but after I read it, I had pretty much learned English."

He finished at the top of his class, got a scholarship to the University of Connecticut and earned an engineering degree. Then he went to the Massachusetts Institute of Technology, where he spent four years earning a doctorate in nuclear physics.

By then an expert in nuclear fusion, he got a job at the Draper Laboratory, a private research organization in Cambridge, designing controls for atomic power plants.

Last September, he took the step for which everything else had been preparation. He applied to the National Aeronautics and Space Administration for the job of astronaut. He got it.

After a year of training, Chang will be a flight specialist, the scientist who conducts experiments, takes charge of the food supply and builds structures outside the spaceship.

The first experimental shuttle flight is scheduled for next March, and NASA hopes the crafts will be making 40 or 50 flights a year by late in the decade.

About three weeks before this book went to press, I met Franklin Chang and had dinner with him. And as we talked I realized again the unbelievable power a dream can have to lead us to our goals—even against incredible odds.

After going through the process we've been discussing a few times—succeeding or failing—some people can begin to sense in a unique way what is do-able and what to expect as they approach new dreams. They will have the experience of being subconsciously steered in the right direction, so that their dreams can emerge clearly and move in a realistic direction.

Of course, those starting into their first venture may have to depend more heavily on the experience of others in checking out their dreams.* But at the beginning stages I cannot emphasize enough that I think one should cut loose and daydream alone, freely and expansively, without being self-critical—the

* See chapter 15 on Experience.

way a child dreams of being a great football player or a movie star or President of the United States.

Dreams can be trimmed to fit reality through the process we'll look at in subsequent chapters. But the tragedy in many lives—and in many business careers—is that people do not dream big enough, or they keep squelching or minimizing their dreams by thinking of reasons why their ideas wouldn't work. This kind of crippling thinking can be compared to a potentially great oak tree that is choked to death in an undersized window pot.

Throughout this discussion about fantasy-dreaming, I have referred to it as a creative process. My psychologist friends tell me that neither scientists nor business educators know much about *how* creativity works. But from what I can gather, something like the dreaming I have described here is a part of the development of all substantial creative ventures.

After dreaming and perhaps being captivated by a prospective venture, the question for the dreamer then becomes, "When do I take a dream out of my mind and plant it in the soil of the real world?" Or, "How do I recognize a *real* opportunity?"

Chapter 7

RECOGNIZING THE OPPORTUNITY

There are dozens of creative opportunities around us all the time—new jobs, chances to get additional education, opportunities to start new businesses or to make changes where we are. But because we have not been trained to look for them, these opportunities are often invisible—though right under our noses. Sigmund Freud discovered that if he asked someone to look up toward the sky and report what they saw, that even though there was a high-flying bird above them, the person would not usually see it. But if Freud said, "Look at that bird," the other person would see it at once—although Freud had not pointed in either case. It seems that in many situations we only see what we are specifically looking for. I think this may be especially true when it comes to seeing important opportunities which might fulfill our lives. Most of us just don't look for significant opportunities.

Because my own vocational experience has been in business, some of the illustrations in this chapter may not seem relevant to you if you are not a business person. But I hope you will stay with me and try to translate the experience of recognizing an opportunity into your own area of excitement and interest, because I am convinced that the process one goes through and the inner attitude that is required in fully recognizing an opportunity are the same in almost any field—regardless of the apparent lack of opportunity in one's situation. Sometimes, in fact, in situations where new options seem to be rather limited, people recognize specific opportunities to fulfill their dreams in their present situations.

For instance, one of the most productive and fulfilled persons I've ever known is a doorman named Bill who has worked at the Shamrock Hilton Hotel in Houston for twenty-five years. Bill has an alertness and sense of being at ease with himself and his work that caught my attention. Every morning he greets all the hotel guests with enthusiasm. And he works long hours; when he isn't on duty as the doorman, he cuts the grass and helps maintain the grounds.

As I talked to Bill during the several months I lived at the Shamrock Hilton, I discovered that he had chosen his career as a part of the larger goals he had set for his whole life. He had wanted his kids to have all of the education they needed to prepare for life. His pride was in full bloom when he discussed his children, who had graduated from college, and one daughter in particular, who was in medical school. Years before Bill had recognized an opportunity to consolidate several smaller jobs around the hotel into a career in which he could meet his life's goals. He was apparently happy and enjoyed the career he had carved out for himself at the Shamrock.

As I think about Bill and the way he combined and transformed pieces of what could be a dull and oppressive life into a productive and creative vocation, I recall other people I know who have shaped large financial and professional careers by being alert to opportunities that came their way. But how? What is involved in recognizing an opportunity when it occurs?

Importance of the American Free Enterprise System

Although it seems obvious, many people do not stop to realize that the basic, and absolutely essential, condition for vocational opportunities as we know them to even *exist* is the free enterprise system itself. And this is true of almost any opportunity requiring freedom of choice and movement. There may be certain advantages to more controlling approaches to enterprise than ours in America, but unless people have the basic freedom to change jobs when they want to, to get more education as they want it, to decide to start a new business or produce a new program or product without severe restrictions, the process I am describing has no air to breathe. The source of creative enterprise and the scene of its activity is a free nation which allows people the freedom to seek and reach their own personal goals.

Recently I was talking to a friend who had just visited the Soviet Union. In discussing the differences in lifestyles between a Russian citizen and an American, my friend reminded me that a Russian cannot just go out and buy an apartment or home the way we do. He has to make application for an apartment, which sometimes takes several months or years to be approved. Once the application is approved, the citizen must live in that particular dwelling until he has received permission to move to another.

My friend also mentioned the fact that, at the completion of the educational process in Russia, students are told where they will go to work. This might involve going to an entirely different city from the one they would prefer. Under this kind of a system there is really no opportunity, as we know it, to change a particular vocation, let alone select the city in which to pursue that career. I'm repeating this with such emphasis because freedom of decision and movement are absolute necessities for vocational opportunities to be recognized and acted upon.

Realizing the Need for Goods or Services

One of the first steps in recognizing an opportunity is the realization that there is a product which is desired, a psychological need to be met, or a service to be rendered. At this point I am not going to discuss the actual steps one goes through to judge whether or not a potential opportunity is financially viable—although later I will describe a way to set concrete goals and formulate action plans to see if the venture is going to fly. At this early stage I only want to point out the importance of a sensitivity to public unrest, needs, and desires which involve producible goods and/or services which are not being adequately produced or rendered.

The entrepreneur "recognizes the opportunity" as he or she envisions himself/herself in a business or vocational position that can be established which will meet the need or provide the service adequately. A classic example of this recognition of need on a very large scale is the Japanese manufacture of small cars with high gasoline mileage. At first American companies refused to retool and produce competitive small cars—until they were almost driven out of the marketplace.

Thirty years ago Jarrell McCracken in Waco, Texas, saw that people had trouble getting good religious music. He recognized an unusual opportunity, and started Word Records, which has become the largest religious record company in the world.

On a more personal level, I know of a woman who, when her children were almost grown, began to have some personal difficulties coping. She was from an upper middle class family and had all the money and social advantages she could want, but was very unhappy. After some hesitation she went to a psychological counseling clinic. There she not only received a great deal of help but discovered how many people like herself needed counseling and that there was a great lack of competent counselors. She recognized an opportunity which captured her imagination, checked it out, talked to her family, went to graduate school for four years, and is now a practicing psychological counselor.

The Attitude of the Innovator in Facing an Opportunity

What goes on inside the mind and heart of a person as he or she confronts what appears to be a viable potential opportunity? What is his/her attitude or emotional state—as opposed to that of an economist or sociologist who is viewing the same set of circumstances?

To recognize an opportunity I believe one must be *in a certain state of mind.* The creative innovator not only recognizes the factual situation, but, even though he or she may not show it, he/she also *gets excited about what is "seen."* There is envisioned not only a potential profit or service, but a whole adventure involving forming a business or providing a product or service that will meet the specific needs of potential users.

I will never forget the sense of excitement and anticipation I felt as I realized the possibility of building a national solid waste company. In my mind far more was involved than a business deal. This may seem like an overstatement, but I think it's a crucial factor in recognizing an opportunity. When looking at a new possibility, a creative innovator's state of mind is a little like that of a boy imagining "going on an adventure to find gold in the jungle along the Amazon."

The reason this attitude of adventure is so important is that it—along with desire—provides the momentum needed to overcome the fear of failure. It has been my experience that I and other people I've known have an incredible amount of fear when it comes to actually putting our careers or egos on the line. *The idea of making a fool out of ourselves is frightening.*

I have already suggested that, because of this fear of rejection and failure, we often allow ourselves to become locked into our present familiar circumstances—even if we are in fact very dissatisfied and longing to reach out in new directions. We tend to become "comfortable" in our dissatisfaction. This is as true for homemakers, managers, and department heads who see creative opportunities *within* their organizations as it is for those looking toward potential opportunities in new contexts. And even if we are looking, these same fears often keep us from looking *far enough* into potential ventures to see whether they have our names on them. But a sense of excitement and adventure can keep us moving forward long enough to investigate the opportunity and see if we want to make a decision to pursue it.

Getting Serious about the Opportunity

After recognizing the need for a product or service with a potential profit (if it's a business) and the fact you could be the one to undertake the adventure, you will have to ask yourself questions like, "Of all the options open to me now, is *this* the one I want to commit *the next chapter of my life* to?" This question is necessary because, at least for a while, after investigating the opportunity and making a decision, your desire and commitment must be focused entirely on the journey to reach the ultimate goal.

Really significant opportunities require a commitment of this magnitude from at least one person (often many others), so along the way family and associates become involved in the outcome of the deliberations. But at this very early stage of investigating, I have a strong personal preference for keeping an idea to myself. This seems to build a strength within me which may be necessary for the follow-through stages.

I really think there is something more to this preference than just my own personal style. When you tell another person about an idea you have, he or she may give you some sort of approval, affirmation, or other positive reinforcement for stating the idea. This verbal feedback may provide you with an immediate feeling of success. If this experience comes too early, and before a real commitment to "go" has been made, you may feel rewarded—as if you had already accomplished the goal. When this happens, desire often subsides, and many times the idea will just drift down the river and never really move from the first recognition into what I call "the action plan."

There is another advantage to keeping the idea a secret at this stage: I think it is dangerous to risk rejection by others until you are fully informed and can defend your idea or plan. Often it will seem that hundreds of people come out of the woodwork of your life just to find all kinds of things wrong with what you are doing or want to do. But after the necessary investigation and planning have been done and you are actually committed to go ahead on the deal, you will not be so vulnerable to negative or contrary opinions.

A Private Awareness That You Are Responsible

Once an idea is born, once a new adventure is perceived, there is a pleasant feeling of discovery accompanied by a fantasy of success. But then, as you think about what may have to be done to make the dream happen, you may begin to feel very uncomfortable. The realization surfaces that if a serious commitment is made, it will be *your* responsibility to move this discovery from an idea to a reality. Even at this very early stage of the decision-making process, a very hard, cold, uneasy, and lonely feeling develops. And it will probably return several times before the final decision is made.

Although I've never read anything about these feelings, I am convinced from my own experience and what others have told me that this loneliness and the fears that leap on us as we experience it represent a very natural, an almost to-be-expected phenomenon in the process we are discussing. I see this sense of aloneness and the awareness of responsibility for one's dreams in ordinary people I've known and in the careers of historical figures as diverse as Moses, Caesar, St. Paul, Sigmund Freud, Madame Curie, Douglas MacArthur, Dag Hammarskjöld, and Golda Meir.

I have found that the only way to adequately deal with this loneliness is to face it. And I believe that this solitary recognition of responsibility, and of the willingness to assume it, needs to take place before the "recognition of an opportunity" can be said to have properly begun.

The Right Combination of Circumstances

Another aspect of seeing and accepting an opportunity has to do with recognizing the unique *relatedness* of several seemingly disconnected circumstances. In 1966, I found in myself a real desire to start a business of my own, just as our subdivision needed someone to collect its garbage. Although I had almost no financial resources, I'd just met a good banker from whom I could borrow some money. There was also the fact that the garbage business I was looking at provided for ninety days advance billing. Although there might have been other opportunities available to me at that time, there were not many in which I could start an entire business with confidence, enthusiasm, a given market, and what appeared to be adequate working capital—when I had such limited funds.

Later, when I recognized the larger opportunity of building a national company, there were other related circumstances which together seemed to constitute almost an invitation from destiny to move forward: The enormous national increase in solid waste, the need for expansion capital in the industry, the fact that many of the owners had illiquid estates with potentially crippling estate taxes, the competition the owners felt from emerging larger companies, the sense of fragmentation in the industry, and the changes in federal laws with regard to the disposal of solid waste.

Because the combination of who I was, what my interests and goals were, and where I was living when the waste industry came to my attention, I had an ideal perspective from which to look at this one particular industry and recognize a major opportunity.

Another example of someone recognizing opportunity through a combination of conditions took place at the end of the Second World War. The failure of world leaders to deal creatively with each other, as well as the specter of Hitler and his "inhuman" tactics, had punctured the easy humanistic optimism which had been prevalent in many churches and synagogues. Just at this time the medium of television was being developed. A young evangelist saw that people were curious about the ultimate questions of life and wanted to relate personally to a God of integrity and caring morality. Billy Graham felt a special call to be used to meet this need and stepped into the opportunity. He has spoken to more people about God than any person in history.

I know a woman in Houston who, fifteen years ago, realized that a rapidly increasing number of women either were becoming successful business or professional people or were receiving inheritances or divorce settlements, and that many of them didn't know anything about handling or investing money. With a great deal of tenacity during a time when it was very difficult for women to have credibility in the financial world, Venita Van Caspel studied, worked, and developed her business. Now she has an enormously successful brokerage firm and has counseled hundreds of women and men concerning how best to use their money to meet their financial goals. She recognized a unique opportunity in the changing circumstances of our time.

But there are usually hundreds of people who at any given time recognize conditions which could form a real business or vocational opportunity. The thing which often separates the successful adventurers from the armchair conversationalists is a certain awareness that a "critical moment" has arrived. This "awareness" is often called "a sense of timing," and it is the subject of the next chapter.

Chapter 8

TIMING

Recently, when trying to describe the tremendous leverage timing can bring to a situation, a friend said, "A fifty-ton boulder sitting in a field can't be moved by a hundred men. But if you happen to find that same sized boulder just as it is balanced on the edge of a cliff, a child can push it down the mountain with a single shove. A sense of timing is the recognition that you've got a boulder that's ready to move—*just when a dragon is coming up the mountain toward you.*" That may be a little simplistic, but it is true that timing is often crucial in the success of a creative effort.

Frequently, people talk about "good fortune" or the role of "luck" in business. In one sense timing depends on luck, but there are almost always potentially "lucky" circumstances around. The trick is to recognize the relatedness of the circumstances *in time to put them together creatively and get an envisioned effect.* For instance, let's say the child on the cliff puts together the idea that the boulder is teetering on the edge and that the dragon charging up the wall of the cliff is in the perfect position to be crushed by the stone. Only if the child *immediately* pushes the boulder and kills the dragon has he taken advantage of a timing opportunity. And although we might say that this is luck, I believe that what people call "luck" is often actually a highly developed, though sometimes unconscious, sense of timing.

Some Components of Timing

Some of the things which make up what I am calling "timing" are awareness, perceptiveness, and the willingness to seriously investigate an apparent opportunity—combined with the guts to step up and commit yourself when you realize you have found an opportunity "with your name on it." Often people have recognized that they are faced with sound opportunities, but haven't been aware of how to pursue them or haven't been willing to "take possession" of an opportunity when the moment to do so has arrived.

Once a timing opportunity is past, it is often gone forever. It seems that there is an optimum moment to respond, and when that moment is past, the clarity of vision fades and the elements which were working together seem somehow scattered and unrelated. And although there are second chances, the odds of getting the identical elements of a significant opportunity in place again are usually pretty remote.

For example, on December 7, 1941, the Japanese in a surprise attack on Pearl Harbor dealt what appeared to be a mortal blow to the United States Navy and came away virtually unscathed. Japan was armed to the teeth; America, in a state of massive confusion and alarm, lay relatively undefended. For a few days, or even weeks, the Japanese could have attacked the United States and perhaps made it impossible for us to develop and deploy the massive war machine which would ultimately defeat them. But they missed that timing opportunity—and lost the war.

Can Large Timing Opportunities be Made?

The question sometimes arises, "Can you *make* good timing opportunities?" I don't think so, at least not as a rule or with major projects. I think the successful innovator has somehow trained himself—or been trained—to look for "boulders near the edge of the cliff." In other words, timing, rather than being something one *causes*, is more often a sudden or gradual awareness that the various parts of a potential opportunity are *al-*

ready in some way related to each other. And timing takes place when the situation seems to be calling for a decision or single act which will bring the components together and start them in motion in a desired direction.

My being president of a suburban civic club with a garbage problem, the federal legislation which eliminated open burning at garbage dumps, Lou Waters's move to Houston—all the components of a national company began to appear to me along with an urgent sense that *"now"* was the time to act.

As I think about the amazing way the lives of the various people and companies involved in the development of BFI came together at the right time, I become increasingly convinced of the substantial role timing plays in the process of developing a large business venture.

Timing Must Include Decisive Action

But timing is not magic, and is of value only when an entrepreneur *acts on his perception*. And this is the whole point of timing. The fact that a big game hunter has the tiger in his scope is important to the hunt only *if* he pulls the trigger . . . while the tiger is still present.

But, even if the timing is ideal, there are several other crucial elements in the creative enterprise process, elements which can *and must be* organized and planned if the opportunity is to move out of the starting blocks toward a successful outcome.

Even with a great opportunity, a heart full of desire, and a sense that the timing is right, the entrepreneur must turn the initial raw opportunity into a workable mass through setting some concrete goals and designing a specific action plan.

Chapter 9

IDENTIFYING LONG-TERM AND SPECIFIC GOALS

This is a difficult chapter for me to write in some ways, since I have always had a lot of resistance to the notion of "setting goals for my life." I like to assume that everything is going to turn out all right and then just hang loose so as to be able to take advantage of new opportunities which come my way. Goal-setting has always seemed like a rigid and uncreative way to live.

But recently I have realized something that has startled me and yet made it clear why I have resisted setting "life" goals. I have come to understand that most people *already have* life goals which they are trying to achieve. But for many of us these goals are *unconscious*—perhaps because of the fear that if we faced our true goals and set out to achieve them, we might fail. (Then what would we do?) So, if our true goals are not conscious, we often feel a confusing conflict about our jobs—and even seem to sabotage our work in order *not* to succeed. And that may be because our unconscious goals are in conflict with our present job or vocation. So I now believe that in many cases the task of "goal-setting" (in terms of our *whole lives*) should be concerned with *identifying* what our life goals *already are.*

For instance, Keith Miller tells me that for years he secretly wanted to be a writer but wouldn't face this because he was afraid he'd fail. His conscious vocational goal was to be a successful oil operator. Then, after fifteen years in the oil business, when he was thirty-eight years old, he wrote a book. When the book came out, he realized that his real goal for years had been to be a communicator. So he quit the oil business and began trying to achieve his true life's goal. Now the setting of smaller goals is no longer a problem for him, because of his discovery of the overall vocational direction he wants to go.

Business or vocational goals are *concrete aims* within one's large life goals. In this chapter we'll look at the advantage of identifying these large life goals *prior to* jumping into the development of a new business or vocation. In the next chapter, I'll describe the process of getting one's personal financial house in order before taking on a new business or vocational goal. And then we'll talk about a way to plan in order to reach these goals.

But first, what are some of the advantages to being aware of your true goals.

A Partial Cure for Indecision

Some of the most agonizing times in my life have been those periods when I was wrestling with an important decision I felt had to be made, but I just could *not* decide and then move on. When times of indecision come, I tend to get in a mental fog and forget or neglect important things in other parts of my life. And until the decision is made my whole life sometimes feels frustrated and directionless.

At such times I feel a little like a person lost in the jungle without a map. I can't see or experience much that is around me because my attention is tunneled on trying to make "my decision." Anyone who has ever gotten married, left a secure job to go on his or her own, gotten a divorce, or decided to sign his life away on a huge note to start a business venture may well recall feeling these paralyzing doubts. At such times I'm tormented by anxious feelings, a tight chest, sweaty palms, and sometimes a sense of confusion—all signs of the fear that I will fail if I make the decision I believe should be made. Indecision can be a particularly draining kind of hell, whether one is a businessperson, a homemaker, or a general in the army.

The other side of the coin for me is that when I have finally *made* an important decision, I feel a great flood of relief and a delightful sense of freedom. I can see the sky again and the people around me; I can smell the rain and laugh. And life feels orderly again.

The making of a hard decision ends a period of inner conflict. And often, once the decision has been made, the energy consumed in wrestling with the alternatives and the fear is released to be used in getting on with living.

All my life I have noticed that some people seem to make decisions easily while others always appear to be slogging through the swamp of indecision. For years, I thought the people who could make good decisions quickly were the strong ones and those who seemed to be always in the process of deciding were the weak ones. But I no longer believe this is necessarily true. Now I have come to see that decision-making is more a matter of *goal clarification* than of personal strength.

Some people's life goals are so clear to them that they can easily say "no" to opportunities which don't relate to reaching those goals. A friend of mine recently told me about a boy he grew up with. It seems that this boy's father owned a building materials company and hoped his son would follow him in the business. But while in the third grade the boy decided he wanted to be a veterinarian. From that time on—and the "boy" is now in his fifties—the dream and occupation of being a veterinarian absorbed Dr. William Chandler. As far as his friends knew, Chandler almost totally avoided the agonizing questions most people have to face in late adolescence and early adulthood as they decide what they are going to do with their lives.

But people who do not have such conscious and specific goals for their lives have to consider and weigh every opportunity, option, or invitation when it comes along. This means that the person without clear long-range goals must spend a great deal more time and energy in the whole process of decision-making.

The "Economy" of Making Overall Decisions

During the past few years I have been living according to the process I am describing in this book. And I have found out something which has given me a whole new sense of freedom and hope about living a happier and more productive life. I have discovered that by making some specific *overall* decisions about the use of my time and abilities, I automatically eliminate an amazing number of smaller decisions. By deciding on the major vocational direction I want to take, I can avoid having to consider a number of major vocational possibilities.

For example, once I had decided to build a large solid-waste company, offers to take a managerial position in any other industry were automatically rejected. If I hadn't established a definite goal, I'd have had to at least consider some offers which came along. And that would have taken a lot of time and energy I needed for my own business.

Besides, once I make a large directional decision, I seem to have more emotional energy to make the tough smaller decisions which are an inevitable part of living. And I am freed to be more creative in all of my life.

Sometimes building a business or developing a vocation by yourself can be very lonely and discouraging. I find that it's easy to lose track of where I'm going and feel as if I have failed—sometimes even when the overall situation is going very well. Having long-term goals for my life which are bigger than any current project makes it easier to keep a perspective, to realize that I really am headed somewhere down the road. It helps me know that, if the current venture doesn't go well, my world won't collapse and there will be other ways to achieve my larger goals.

Determining Your Goals—a Case History

A man I've known for years used to say laughingly when I was a boy, "Tom, if you don't know where you're going, how in the world are you going to know when you get there?" He was expressing a simple but profound psychological truth. Whether it is a little girl finishing a challenging puzzle, a grown-up running a marathon, or a member of a management group acquiring a hundred companies, there seems to be a common need in people of all ages to accomplish goals. This desire to actualize specific dreams is a great motivator for long-term performance and satisfaction. And life goals on the horizon can give one a continuing sense of direction in spite of vocational and personal roadblocks and detours.

In the process of writing this book, Keith and I have talked many hours about the different kinds of power and freedom we're finding as we identify our goals and do action plans to achieve them. As a result, Keith has begun consulting with people who feel a lack of direction in midlife, helping them identify goals and design action plans for meeting those goals. The following account in his own words is taken from a series of interviews with a man seeking a new vocational goal:

Will Brandon is a forty-nine-year-old man who has a college degree in mechanical engineering and who is the sole owner of a respected engineering company employing about twenty people. Will is a very intelligent, nice-looking man with an attractive wife and three sons who are all grown, out of college, and on their own. His business has not been doing well financially. That's not surprising, though, since he doesn't like engineering. He'd much rather sell the business and do something else, but he doesn't know what he'd like to do or how he'd begin at his age. He heard I'd been doing some work concerning the identifying of vocational goals, and asked me to help him.*

We got together and talked for about an hour about Will's present situation. He seemed vague and uncertain about any positive direction for the future, but was quite specific about the things in his situation he didn't like. I asked him if he had any idea what his overall goal in life was. He thought a few seconds and said very definitely, "No question—peace of

---

* In this account, the names and several of the basic circumstances are changed to protect the privacy of those involved. But the basic components of Will's situation are unchanged.

mind." But he didn't have any ideas about how to reach that goal. I took Will through the following procedure to help him discover his goals for the rest of his life and to settle on a particular vocational goal.

I told him to take a legal pad and a pencil (with an eraser), and write his overall life goal on the top of the page. He wrote, "Peace of Mind." Then I asked him to quickly list all the things which he could imagine would contribute to the peace of mind he wanted. When he'd finished, he studied the list a few minutes and added several more items.

*His completed list looked like list #1, below:**

Peace of Mind

1. *Vocation—accomplishment in business*
2. *Being loved and approved of by Jane and the boys*
3. *Financial security*
4. *Four weeks vacation per year*
5. *Taking some three-day weekends*
6. *Getting in shape physically*
7. *Health*
8. *Time alone*
9. *Being in control of my vocation*
10. *Stature in the community*
11. *Active role in the church*
12. *Time with friends*
13. *Trip to Paris and London (sometime)*

After making sure he didn't want to add anything else (I assured him that he could add others later), I told Will that

---

* If you are interested in trying this procedure, you will need a pencil and a pad. You may come up with a single goal, as Will did (e.g., to be happy). In that case, list all the things you can think of which would help reach that goal (make you happy). Many people state several life goals right off (e.g. financial security, time with family, to be an outstanding pianist). If you have more than one, these several goals can constitute the beginning of your list #1, since what you are trying to determine with this list are the things which would fulfill your life. Add to these items any other goals you can think of, and your list #1 will be completed.

now we at least had a concrete picture of all the elements which he felt could help him meet his life goal. If he could figure out a way to meet these thirteen life goals during the next few years, he would be taking concrete steps toward a more fulfilling life.

Then I asked Will to quickly rank the thirteen goals on his list in terms of their (honest) priority to him. His revised list is shown in list #2:

Goals toward Peace of Mind

1. *Vocation—accomplishment in business*
2. *Approval from Jane and boys*
3. *Health*
4. *Being in control of my vocation*
5. *Financial security*
6. *Active role in church*
7. *Stature in the community*
8. *Time alone*
9. *Time with friends*
10. *Trip to Paris and London*
11. *Getting in shape physically*
12. *Four weeks vacation per year*
13. *Taking some three-day weekends*

*With the completion of this revised list, we had something to go on in determining how Will could meet his life's goals. It was important to rewrite the list in this order so Will could see (in black and white) just what his priorities were.**

Since Will's first concern was his unhappy vocational situation, I suggested that we examine his vocational possibilities. *He took a clean sheet of paper and wrote "Vocational Possibili-*

---

* This same process of identifying one's true goals will often work with an institution—like a church, foundation, or service organization—which finds itself fuzzy about its specific major goals. I once led a church congregation through this process. Together at a special meeting they listed and prioritized their goals for the church. From that point they were able to make specific plans to reach each goal.

ties" at the top. On this page he listed every possible vocational position or venture which really appealed to him—regardless of whether they seemed feasible or impossible. *His list is below:*

Vocational Possibilities

1. *Consultant concerning operating a business*
2. *Operations manager—V.P. for large corporation*
3. *P.R. man for large corporation*
4. *Commercial realtor—putting together deals to build hotels, condominiums and residences*
5. *New business developer for a large corporation*
6. *Consultant—for new product development*
7. *Stockbroker—investment counselor*

When he had ranked his vocational possibilities in terms of their priority to him, the list looked like this:

1. *Commercial realtor—putting together deals to build hotels, condominiums and residences*
2. *Consultant—business*
3. *Investments—broker*
4. *Consultant—new product development*
5. *P.R. for large corporation*
6. *Operations manager*
7. *New business developer for large corporation*

Next we talked about his first choice: being a commercial realtor. We looked at list #1 to see if he could imagine meeting his life goals in this business. He could imagine meeting them all. As we talked, Will really began to get excited. At last he had uncovered what he really wanted to do. He had a vocational goal, and he understood better what his true life goals were and how his new vocational goal related to them.

Next Will designed an action plan (see chapter 13) to discover how he could get to be a commercial realtor. He is in the midst of checking that plan as these words are being writ-

ten, and he seems like a man on a very positive and happy adventure.

If, after checking his action plan, Will discovers that it will be impossible for him to be a commercial realtor, he can do another action plan to find out about his second choice—being a business consultant. But by following this process Will is no longer stuck and dissatisfied; he is aware of his life goals and is taking concrete action to find out what he really can do vocationally. And if, after checking all his vocational choices, Will finds that he can only *do what he is already doing (this is very unlikely), at least he'll have the satisfaction of knowing that,* according to his own investigation, *he is in the only job that is feasible for him.*

After Keith had helped Will find a vocational goal, he had Will do a study of his personal finances, to make sure he could move forward to investigate the commercial real estate business and locate *specific* commercial real estate ventures. (In the next chapter, we will discuss how to carry out such a financial study.) But, for now, Will had a new vocational goal, and a lot of enthusiasm generated by seeing what that goal could mean to the other goals in his life.

Although it is sometimes more complex, this process of stating all the desirable options and ranking them in terms of priority to you is helpful in setting goals in all sorts of situations. It is a way for a creative person to quickly get a feel for the kinds of goals that are really important to him or her. And since all of the goals and options are suggested by the *one seeking* to clarify his or her situation, the motivation to move forward toward the goals is often very strong.

When you have done the investigation of your own life goals the way Keith helped Will do, you can check any new creative opportunity that comes along against them. This will let you see whether the new deal will help you meet most of your long-term goals or simply frustrate you.

For instance, nine of Will's goals are directly related to his vocational life. If he was offered a job that allowed for no active role in his church, no real control of his vocation, no time alone, only a one-week vacation, no three-day weekends, and no particular stature in his community, he'd suspect it was a bad long-term venture for him to get into, even if it offered a *tremendous amount* of financial security. (Incidentally, when Will checked his engineering-company work against his thirteen life goals, he found that he was meeting only *two!*) It is important to see that identifying your life goals can give some solid criteria that must be met before you will even consider a new activity or venture.

Specific Goals

A specific vocational goal (as opposed to a life goal) is a definite, definable project or objective, the accomplishment of which can be easily measured by the person who sets the goal. To get a Ph.D. in physics could be a specific goal, or to save ten-thousand dollars. To build a profitable men's clothing business or a large multicity garbage company, or to quit one's job with a large company and become a free-lance writer—all these are examples of possible specific vocational goals. And of course, any specific vocational goal one sets should be compatible with and lead toward the accomplishment of one or more life goals.

Remember, too, that large vocational goals are made up of many small goals. For instance, before one can get a Ph.D. he or she must usually graduate from high school and college. Each of these smaller goals must be accomplished before reaching the larger goal of earning a Ph.D.

Specific vocational goals can be the result of personal decisions—for instance, becoming a professional writer. Or they can be required by an organization—salespersons are often given a quota-goal to reach in a given period of time. But in any case, in order for the creative enterprise process to work, a person must learn how to set specific goals and meet them.

Choosing Goals

Very early in my business career, it became clear to me that, if I intended to take goals seriously, there were a couple of very important things I'd have to remember:

(1) Since I was going to be committed to *reaching* the specific goals I set, I'd have to be very careful in *choosing* them. Before making a firm decision about committing to accomplish a goal, I'd have to be sure I had an action plan which would really move me to that goal (see chapter 13). For the sake of credibility with one's associates and oneself, it is bad to form a habit of abandoning goals one has decided to achieve. Besides, large amounts of money and emotional energy are wasted every year by people failing to accomplish goals. And many of these people never had a chance, given the lack of feasible routes toward reaching their goals—routes which were never properly investigated.

(2) The second "essential" I learned very early about goal-setting is that it is extremely important not to have *too many* goals. When this has happened to me, I have been continually frustrated and felt fragmented, as if there were never enough hours in a day to get things done. I will never forget the agony of trying to run the garbage business, work in my accounting firm, and help a friend start a new business—all in the 1966 tax season. Now, as difficult as it is to do sometimes, I try to limit my major goals to a very few at any one time.

Since goal-setting may change the course of your life, I urge you to take plenty of time before committing to large vocational or personal goals. Another reason it is important to consider goals carefully is that there is built into most of us an enormous and fearful resistance to any change which involves risk. We are afraid that if we change we might fail. And any uncertainty about the goals you set out to achieve can substantially increase this built-in fear of failure.

It takes courage to establish serious goals—and then to set out to meet them. So when you are face to face with a vocational opportunity, make sure you have the staying power to check the deal thoroughly. Check the proposed goal against your life goals. But also check your present financial situation, to see what kind of assets and requirements you would bring with you into the new venture.

Chapter 10

PERSONAL FINANCIAL PLANNING FOR MEETING GOALS

There are many ways to use the creative enterprise process within your present job or occupational setting without causing any change, at least immediately, in your personal finances. For example, an employee of a business or other institution might set new sales or departmental production goals that would bring about tremendous improvement in a particular part of the larger organization. But in this chapter I am going to assume that the new goal you have set for your life will drastically affect both the source and the amount of your income.

In planning your strategy for dealing with this change, you will first need to determine the precise amount of income you can count on from present sources if you quit the job you have now. In addition, you will need to carefully calculate what your financial needs will be. And then, if your needs exceed the amount of income presently available, you will need to set plans in motion to make up the difference. By settling the matter of your immediate needs and possibly modifying your lifestyle to adjust to what is feasible, you will then be free to concentrate your full energy on the achievement of your new business, vocational, or personal goals.

I suggest your financial examination include three steps: (1) examining your present financial situation to determine fixed obligations and expenses and the income you can depend on if you make the change, (2) deciding on the minimum standard of living you could be comfortable with during the investigation and building period, and (3) devising a plan to arrange for obtaining sufficient money for your support while you are setting out to accomplish your new goal.

Examining Your Present Financial Situation

The purpose of the first step in the financial inventory is to give yourself a clear picture of how much additional money you will need to come up with from outside sources during the investigation of your dream. This information will also tell you how much you will need during the "building period" if you decide to commit yourself to that particular goal. (Of course, as a part of this step, you will have to estimate how long it will take you to get the new venture to the point that it can provide all the money for your expenses.)

To survey your financial situation, first go through your current financial books and list the following:

(1) *Every financial obligation you anticipate having during the next year.* Include house payment, food, education, clothing, any investment loans, taxes—every conceivable expense, with a percentage included to allow for inflation. If your vocational goal will involve additional preparation, education, or training, any related expense should be included—and the time extended as necessary.

(2) *Every known income stream.* Write down any form of income that would still be available to you if the change requires selling your business or quitting your job (include interest income, etc.).

(3) *Every disposable asset* except your home and automobile. Include savings and a quick sale estimate for any business or other property you may presently own.

When you have finished these lists and totaled the figures, you will have a clear picture of your estimated expenses for the next year, your estimated continuing income for the next year (without present salary or income from present vocation), and your debts (and assets with which to service or liquidate them). Subtract the income and disposable assets from the expenses to see how much additional income you will need.

Let's say that upon completion of these computations you came up with an estimated income of ten thousand dollars for next year and expenses of thirty-five thousand, with saleable assets of fifteen thousand. When you subtract the income (ten thousand) from the estimated expenses (thirty-five thousand), you can see clearly that a minimum of twenty-five thousand dollars is needed during the next year as you move toward your new vocation or business. Of course, if you should decide to sell part or all of your disposable assets, the proceeds from such a sale would also apply against the difference.

I have used a one-year time period here in making this example, but of course you will have to estimate how much time your own venture will take for investigation and startup. Your new goal should of course eventually provide the total income needed for expenses, once the new business or vocation is established.

Deciding on Your Comfort Zone

In working through this process you will have determined clearly how much money you will have to live on during this starting-up process. With this information in hand, you may then need to review your standard of living (with your wife or husband) to see if any cutbacks are possible without intruding unduly on what is required for your basic comfort. By looking at your financial situation this way, you will also know something about what to ask from your new situation and what you can sacrifice while still meeting your (family's) needs.

When I started an accounting firm with two other men in 1966, we decided we would limit our salaries to $750 per month each in order to keep our overhead down for the first year. That was less than we'd been making, but we knew it might be a while before we could generate much income. As things developed, this was a wise decision, since we didn't take in any income at all for the first nine months.

Devising a Plan to Get the Money to Support You While Preparing to Meet Your Goals

When it isn't readily apparent just how a person or a couple can obtain the money needed to live on while moving toward the accomplishment of the new goal, there is the tendency to panic. But very few people can just plunge into this kind of change immediately. So if you are serious about reaching your long-term vocational goals, you must begin to make a concrete plan to clear up past obligations and get the support money you need before you can start working toward your new goals.

I have a good friend who wanted to start a new chapter in his life. He had decided on a particular new business venture and was very excited and eager to get on with it. But after checking his finances he found that he would need a rather large sum of money to bail himself out of his past obligations.

My friend happened to be an outstanding dramatic performer, and although doing one-night engagements was not his favorite way to earn money, he realized that by *loading* his schedule with one-night performances for *two years*, he could clear up his obligations and be ready to pursue his ultimate goals. It was a tough price to pay, but he paid it.

Other people have cut back their standard of living and begun to save while still in their present jobs. Some have taken second jobs. Still others have sought grants or scholarships. It is hard work to carve out space to accomplish desired goals, and it may take one, five, or ten years, but it can usually be done.

If the price I am suggesting here seems too high, you might ask yourself, "What is a fulfilled life worth?" Many people never realize that most men and women who do outstanding things or go for their dreams have paid *long hours* and *even years* of sacrificing to get where they want to go.

In writing this chapter I realize that many people do not feel they have any flexibility or mobility with regard to their particular financial situation. Those who have always worked at just one job often don't realize that in the present economic situation many men and women go into new areas of work every day—often without "adequate" preparation.

I know of a man who is an outstanding speech professor. He's made great contributions to his field for years, but is now approaching early retirement and wants to become a writer. But he didn't know what to do to earn money to support his family while he began to accomplish his new goal. Another friend of his pointed out several ways he could consult in business and teach businesspeople how to communicate more effectively. The professor had never thought of his abilities as being usable outside a college classroom. The suggestion opened up a whole new field of opportunity to him, and he's preparing to embark on an exciting second career as a consultant and writer.

There are often part-time or second jobs that can be a source of extra income. And sometimes there are ways to "moonlight free" toward one's goals. For instance, many young performers have broken into the pop music field by "hanging around" studios and working without compensation. At first it's just a "learning experience," but finally they may get a break.

Waiting to get the income needed for a new goal or vocational venture may be difficult and frightening. And some people are so afraid of not making it that they won't try at all. But my goal here is to communicate with and encourage people with imaginative minds who can visualize change and who have the strong desire to *live* their dreams. I have come to believe that there are thousands upon thousands of people who could be freed from their conditioned restraints by establishing, planning for, and moving toward new vocational goals. And I know from personal experience that the process we're looking at here can work.

Chapter 11

"USING" YOUR GOALS TO REACH YOUR DREAMS

Let's assume you have identified the goals for your life which you believe would bring you satisfaction and happiness. Let's also say that you now have a specific goal in or beyond your present job. It may be starting a new business, restructuring a department, or getting the training necessary to enter a new profession. You have examined your financial situation, if necessary, and are ready to look seriously at what must be done to reach your new goal.

The action plan (next chapter) is a way to coordinate all efforts to reach your stated goals. But in the day-to-day working out of all plans, goal-setting at different levels can become a continuing source of help.

Looking at Goals a Year at a Time

Once a specific vocational goal has been determined, I have found it helpful to set intermediate goals for the year ahead. To do this, first write on a piece of paper all the goals you would like to accomplish in the coming year. At this point you should check to make sure these goals will move you toward the accomplishment of your long-term goals, especially your new vocational goal. (If this is not true, I believe you must scrap the intermediate goals you've just written down. Life is too short to work at cross purposes with your ultimate aims.)

Next, rewrite the list in the order the goals must be accomplished.

Short-Term Goals

The next step is to break down the yearly goals into short-term goals that will assist you in reaching your yearly goals. My first breakdown is usually into *monthly goals,* with specific dates for their accomplishment. Then I take it a step further and set up *weekly goals.* My pattern then is to decide at the first of the week what I can reasonably expect to get done by Friday.

I followed this system of yearly and short-term goals when I was involved in reorganizing a certain company. (My goal for the year was to raise the profits to a desired figure by the end of the next year.) First I did a projection study in October to determine the profit we would need by the end of the next year. After a careful organizational study, we estimated, with the help of our division heads, the profit for which each division could be responsible.

I then proceeded to break down our yearly goal into specific short-term goals and parceled these out to appropriate division heads; by December 10 (before the year started), I wanted from each division specific plans as to how their short-term goals were to be accomplished. Meetings would be held between December 10–20 to examine the plans, adjust them if necessary, and make sure they were coordinated with those of other divisions. The period between January 1 and March 31 would be a time for beginning to implement the plans. Then, during the week of April 1–7, there would be meetings to examine and report on the progress of the plans. In the week of July 1–8 would be another checkpoint, the purpose of which would be to beef up or adjust plans which weren't on schedule. And there would also be meetings September 1–4, October 1–4, and November 1–4 to make sure we were on track.

By setting these goals with definite dates and putting them on my calendar before the first of the year, I and the people with whom I worked in the company had a clear structure and goals to work toward. It is incredible how a little time spent with a calendar, setting annual and monthly goals, can give you a more reality-oriented picture of what you actually can and cannot commit to do in the year ahead.

It took a little while before I could realistically appraise the time necessary for certain tasks—and I still have to adjust continually. But the results as compared to not setting goals are impressive to me. And of course you can always adjust dates on a calendar if you misjudge the time necessary for accomplishing something. But I am just amazed at how *few* have to be changed once they are set on everyone's calendars.

A Decision Regulator

At the beginning of each year I take a three-by-five card and write down my four most important life-long goals, along with my yearly goals. I always carry this card in my pocket, and I refer to it many times a day.

I realize that you may think this is a highly structured and intractable way to live, or that you may envision yourself wandering around lost in a galaxy of different-sized goals. But in my case, at least, the opposite is actually true. For one thing, having my goals written down gives me a sense of structure; I'm much more likely to get my goals accomplished in the midst of the consuming busyness which threatens to engulf so many of us. And because I have my goals *in writing*, my mind isn't cluttered by trying to "remember" them all the time.

In addition, by keeping the major goals on a three-by-five card, I have a powerful decision-making tool with me all the time. Many times, when I'm on the telephone or in a meeting, I pull the card out and ask myself whether what I am doing (or considering doing) is going to help me substantially to accomplish the goals on that card. If the answer is "no," I move away from my present activity as quickly as possible. Surprisingly, this little card is a great help to me when considering any proposed use of my time or resources. There were times, during the two years at BFI when I was arranging the acquisition of more than one company per week, when I wouldn't have been able to remember what I was doing if I hadn't kept a very frequent check on my long-term and short-term goals.

Getting Sidetracked from Your Goals by "Good Deals"

There are a couple of quirks in human nature which keep many people from reaching their goals. One, to which I have already alluded, is our egotistical tendency to think we can do "everything at once." We take on more than we can handle, get anxious, and fail.

But even if our goals are realistic, many of us seem to have a second negative habit: we tend to do self-defeating things, sometimes with no apparent reason except we just "wanted to at the moment." I know a woman who will carefully diet for weeks—and then sit down and eat an entire chocolate cake. It's not rational, but it's very human!

This self-defeating tendency can trip us up as we work toward our long-term goals. Once one identifies his or her life goals and sets a specific business or vocational goal, there is a strong tendency to get sidetracked by other glamorous possibilities for the use of time and money. But doing this can keep even the most talented people from leading fulfilled lives.

I once knew a brilliant young scholar who inherited a large sum of money. Instead of investing the money carefully to provide the freedom he needed to do the research (which was the dream of his life), he participated in a "good deal" with a couple of friends—an investment in a real-estate venture they were jointly responsible for managing. The venture was very successful financially. With his natural managerial talents my friend felt he had to organize and take care of the rapidly expanding business. He had less and less time for his research and for his family.

Several years later he had made a great deal of money but had completely dropped his research—though the desire to get at it plagued him constantly. He had also neglected his family along the way and was divorced. Because of his new financial success, he didn't know whether he could return to the style of life he had followed as a scholar doing research. When he talked about what had happened, he just shook his head and wondered if he'd blown his real chance in life. And he said rather sadly that he really didn't even care about the money. But he'd just been presented with such a good opportunity that he "couldn't turn it down."

Don't misunderstand. If making a lot of money had been this man's long-term vocational goal, he could have been very happy. But he had been diverted from what his real goal was, and in such a powerful way that he may never be able to fulfill the dream of his life.

Saying "no" to good deals is a very hard way to live—especially for an entrepreneur. But if you want to accomplish great things in your life, I know of no other way than to be disciplined in limiting the number and direction of your goals.

Goal-Setting Is Not Enough

Some people read a book or hear a lecture on goal-setting and promptly decide to set goals for their lives. And sadly, for many men and women the act of setting goals is the end of the matter. But the secret of goal-setting is to *actively pursue those goals in a realistic way.*

Once while I was in New York at the offices of a major company, the head of a subsidiary of that company took a three-hundred-page report and threw it on the desk in front of me. He said, "This is our subsidiary's five-year plan. We spent two weeks of management time developing it. But our parent company doesn't want any change, so I'll guarantee that we'll never look at this plan again."

The implication was that even though a lot of creative thought and energy had gone into setting new goals, the business would go on as usual. The feeling I got from this frustrated manager was that in the parent company there was more emphasis on going through the motions of being creative and of setting goals than on moving forward. And the incredible tragedy is that this is true of many companies—and of many individuals.

One reason many people set goals and never pursue them is that they don't know how to design solid plans to insure that their goals have a good chance of being achieved. This lack of know-how, combined with the universal fear of failure, is enough to stop many people from trying new things. But I have discovered that there is an approach to planning which, if followed, will enormously increase your chances of succeeding.

Chapter 12

CONSTRUCTING ACTION PLANS

Action planning is the most valuable tool I have ever found for efficiently accomplishing significant goals. This sort of planning is deceptively simple—a quick and efficient method of breaking difficult projects or tasks down into manageable pieces.

And that's what action planning really is: taking a goal—*any size* goal—and breaking it down into the separate tasks or requirements which will lead to its accomplishment. Each task or requirement then becomes a smaller goal for which a specific action plan can be made. When we finish this process of breaking each goal into smaller goals and devising action plans for each, we have a complete road map which shows the way from the starting point to the final achievement.

Action planning can revolutionize the direction of an individual life, a department within a company, or an entire corporation. And this sort of planning can be used on almost any kind of goal or task, large or small—from writing a speech to changing vocations to outlining the building and operation of a large hotel. Using these three examples, I hope to give a clear picture of how action planning works.*

* There are actually many approaches to efficient planning and meeting specific goals in business. "Management by objectives" is a whole approach to this subject. The methods I have discovered and used will work in many situations, but the explanations and charts presented in this chapter are merely simple models which you may want to use as starting points to design something

Action Planning for Small Goals—Writing a Speech

If I were sitting down to prepare a talk to a group of division managers about the goals for the coming year (e.g., regarding the company plan described in the last chapter), the action planning would go something like this:

(1) *I would list at random every main point I'd like to make.* I would not try to put the points in any order at this time because to do so might block the creative process of getting them all down on paper. The original list might look like this (list #1):

Goal: Speech to Division Heads
on Goals for Next Year

1. Overall goals for next year
2. Sales quotas by division
3. Action plans from each division (with dates)
4. How quotas were arrived at
5. Overall goals—financial goals
6. Affirmation of division heads for present attitude
7. Assurance that we can meet these goals
8. Schedule of deadlines for action plans and performance

(2) The second step (after being sure I cannot think of any other major point I need to make in the speech) is to *reorder the points in a logical order for presentation.* That list would look like this (list #2):

Goal: Speech to Division Heads
on Goals for Next Year

1. Affirmation of division heads for present attitude
2. Overall goals for next year

---

which will fit your own situation. In a very complex business involving a lot of scheduling, there are helpful tools available, like Gantt charts and Pert charts. A much more detailed and technical book describing these and other ways production can be improved to meet one's goals in business is *Production Management,* by Franklin G. Moore and Thomas Hendrick (Homewood, Ill.: Richard D. Irwin, Inc., 1977).

3. Overall goals (broken down into) financial goals
4. Sales quotas by divisions
5. How sales quotas were arrived at
6. Action plans from each division (with dates)
7. Schedule of deadlines for action plans and performance
8. Assurance that we can meet these goals

(3) The third step in this action plan would be to check with any other executives or partners responsible for the next year's goals, to make sure no major points are being left out, and then to *flesh out each of the eight major points* with numbers, dates, and illustrations. (This would mean doing a miniature action plan for each point.)

(4) The final step would be to *check any points I am not sure of* with the proper person in the organization (re: finances, dates of meetings, etc.). Then I would go through each of the eight points and write in my own words what I am actually going to say.

This process may seem cumbersome, but if you are not a born or trained public speaker (as I am not), action planning can save you hours of agony in trying to figure out what to say. You will almost never leave out important points this way, and after you become accustomed to making action plans you will find them amazing time-savers. I planned the above speech (steps one and two) in fifteen minutes.

You may be thinking that the procedure followed in drawing up the action plan is very similar to the one used by Keith to help Will Brandon focus on vocational and life goals. This is no accident, since the basic process of listing possibilities and breaking these down into workable parts is the same in both procedures. But action planning is done with a different purpose; here we are working to determine *how* a specific goal can be accomplished, not what the goal will be.

An Action Plan for a Vocational Change

One great thing about action planning is that by using it you can approach tasks you have never done before and get at the essentials to evaluate their chances of accomplishment with the least wasted effort—and usually without having to commit any large sums of money.

The following is a true account of an action plan drawn up by a married woman friend who had read an earlier draft of this book in 1979. She decided she would investigate the possibility of quitting her job as a marketing director with a company to fulfill a lifelong goal of becoming a free-lance writer.

After doing a personal financial study to determine how much money she would need to provide income for paying debts and taking care of estimated 1980 commitments, she proceeded with formulating an action plan. She reports in her own words the following steps:

First I wrote my goal at the top of a blank sheet of paper and listed quickly all the things I could think of that I'd have to do or know about before I could leave my job and begin writing. I came up with the following (list #1):

Goal: To Become a Writer

1. *Line up projects to write*
2. *Time schedule: when to leave job*
3. *Identify income sources to replace income from full-time job*
4. *Plan daily time management*
5. *Locate place to write and keep files: office*

I then placed these five items in priority order, as follows (list #2):

Goal: To Become a Writer

1. *Identify income sources to replace income from full-time job*
2. *Time schedule: when to leave job*
3. *Locate a place to write and keep files: office*

4. Daily time management
5. Line up projects to write

After prioritizing these different elements, I took item number one, "Income to replace income from full-time job," and wrote that at the top of a clean sheet of paper. I already knew (from doing my financial study) about what I would need to make in order to afford to leave my job, and decided I could get by on a smaller income for a while, if necessary, in order to make the change. Then I listed all the possible income sources I could think of (list #3):

1. Income to replace income from full-time job.
   A. Consulting
      1. Programs/conferences
      2. Time management
      3. Music marketing (my former field)
   B. Group travel (I'd had some experience traveling with tours.)
   C. Speaking (re: women in business, being a single Christian)
   D. Copywriting for advertising companies
   E. Editing
   F. Proofreading
   G. Writing royalties (eventually)

I checked with people in the area of each possible income stream and made estimates as to the amounts I might make. Then I cut the projected amount by one-third to provide room for over-optimistic estimates. When I had done these things, I realized that, although I would be making a smaller income, I could afford to change vocations based on the income possibilities listed above. All of this would give me better control of my time, enabling me to begin to write.

The action plan list for the next item from list #2, "Time schedule: when to leave my job," included such things as giving sufficient notice to my employer, not leaving in the middle of big promotional campaigns, getting a specific offer for consulting, making plans for a group tour to Oberammergau, and getting a contract to write a book for choir directors. I was able to settle on a date for resigning at the company four months ahead of time; this way I could be sure to give one month's advance notice.

Item number three, "Locate a place to write and keep files: office," brought forth a list of things like "location, cost to rent, furniture, equipment, etc."

Item number four, "Daily time schedule," was important to me because of my strong fear of falling into the familiar writer's trap of "not having time to write," even after leaving a full-time job to "devote more time to writing." I needed to feel assured that I could handle the other details of my life and still have ample time for my writing. I did this by deciding on the number of hours I would spend for housekeeping, fitness and health, preparing food, quiet time, writing, and consulting or doing any other work I would need to do to produce the income I needed.

After writing out this list, I negotiated with my husband for a division of the household responsibilities, and we agreed I also needed to hire a part-time maid. By planning a weekly time chart, blocking out specific "office hours" and "writing hours," I felt assured I could live comfortably within the hours I had planned and still take care of the other things I would need to do. Periodic adjustments in the weekly time chart are all that have been necessary to keep a reasonable work flow possible.

After she checked her action plans and found them workable, my friend left her job in the fall of 1979. Making the adjustment has not been easy, but it has paid off: she has completed the writing of one book, is the coauthor of a study course, and is writing a second book, plus doing consulting projects with several different people. And she says that it was during the action planning that she realized she *really could* risk becoming a writer and going after her dream.

Action Planning for Large, Complex Goals

So far we have looked at very simple and straightforward uses of the action plan. But if you have a large, complex goal like building a big business or other institution, action planning is even more crucial to success. In fact, with the increasing complexity and changing costs of things like materials, real estate, labor, products and services, I would consider it close to raw luck to succeed in any really large project without setting concrete goals and drawing up specific action plans (which take into consideration the changing costs and other variable conditions).

For example, let's say that Will Brandon decided to go into commercial real estate and wanted to build and operate a large hotel project. Obviously, the finished action plans for such a venture would take pages to describe. But the principle for each plan would be the same: Will would first have to decide on the overall goal (building and operating a hotel) and list under it the major subgoals which must be reached in order to achieve the larger goal. Next, he would put each subgoal on a separate sheet of paper and determine everything which must be done or obtained in order to accomplish that particular goal. Then, if there were any points he didn't know how to handle on any of these lists, he would make separate sheets and do action plans for them.

Will's first list of major goals might look something like this (list #1):

Primary Goal: Building and Operating a Hotel

1. Financing
2. Complete construction of buildings
3. Establish a trained sales force
4. Develop a management team
5. Plan first year's operation

The items on list #1 are the major subgoals. Each of them would be put on a separate sheet of paper, and everything involved in reaching that goal would be listed, prioritized, and checked. For instance, under the goal, "Complete construction of necessary buildings," would be listed such things as the following (list #2):

2. Complete construction of necessary buildings
    A. Location
    B. Architect—plans
    C. Contractor
    D. Construction time scheduled

Will might then want to make action plans for the items in list #2 by putting each of them at the head of a separate sheet of paper and listing what it would take to get that item done.

This process of breaking down larger goals into smaller, reachable goals and then checking them would continue until Will knew that each small task or goal necessary to reach his primary goal could be accomplished.

When Will finally combined the smaller action plans under each major goal, it would be *very* important for him to estimate *when* each step would be completed, and to put those dates on his calendar (as well as the calendars of anyone else who would be responsible for the project's success). Since the several major goals that make up this project would have to be reached more or less at the same time, the separate timetables for those major goals could then be combined into an overall action plan with coordinated timetables.

Although it may look very complicated at first glance, such a coordination can create a panoramic picture into which adequate resources could be plugged at the proper time with a minimum of waste. Coordinated Action Plan I on p. 110 gives a rough idea of how such an overall panoramic view of all action plans might look on the hypothetical hotel project.

In Action Plan I, each arrow represents a *series* of steps necessary to reach a minor goal, the accomplishment of which is part of reaching a major goal. This is of course a very simplistic and abstract picture. It is included only to give you a notion of how action planning can be used to break down very large

GOAL OF ENTIRE VENTURE
BUILDING AND OPERATING A HOTEL PROJECT

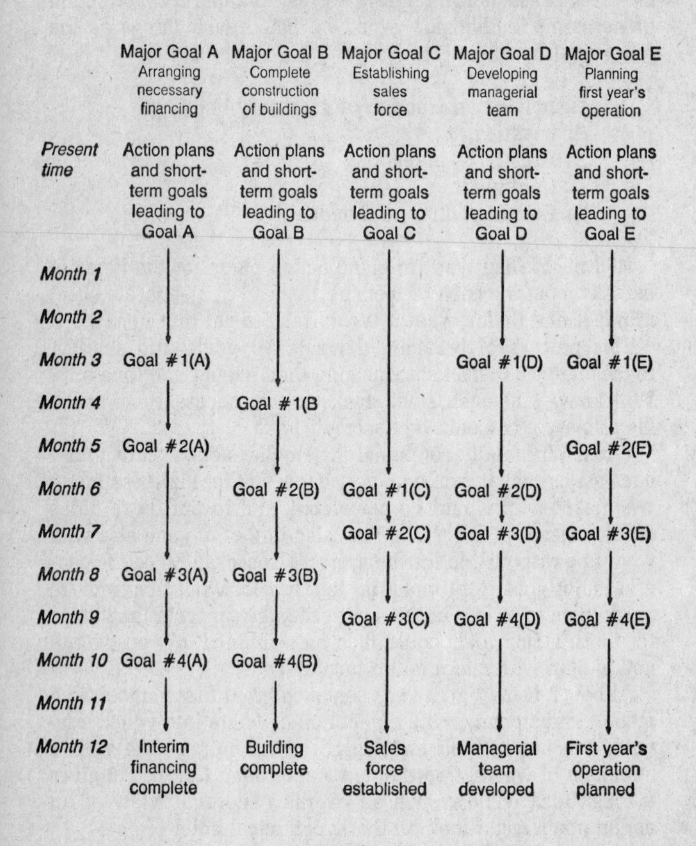

Action Plan I

goals into tasks which can be measured, costed, and totalled *prior* to making a commitment to "go" on a project. Although I have used a business example, the same principles would apply to the building of a school, church, hospital, retail store, insurance company, or other large institution.

Attitude While Action Planning—No Critical Input

At this point in the process, I've found that the attitude of those devising the action plans is very important. There should be *no negative or critical input or feedback while the plans are being devised.* This non-critical freedom allows the creative process to flow, so that the lists and logical breakdown of the goals can come freely and naturally from the person or people doing the planning. They can see the project or business develop quickly before their eyes.

Remember, at this point you are not yet committed; you are in a creative stage of determining the necessary intermediate goals and steps to take toward your larger goal. Of course, there will be discussions if more than one person is doing the planning. But maintaining a positive open atmosphere in which ideas can be "tried on" without being shot down is *very* important. There will be an evaluation and checking process to be entered into *after* the action plans are complete (see next chapter). Then questioning and criticism will be very valuable.

Action planning can be a very exciting experience. It's like painting a picture, and is one of the most enjoyable parts of the creative enterprise process for me. While I am making action plans, there is no possibility of failure, no major blocks—it's all success! And since one of the psychological conditions for creativity is the freedom to fail, action planning in a positive environment can be amazingly creative; plans can be made and tied together unhampered by the blocking power of a negative or critical environment. And my experience would indicate that an unusual percentage of the action plans formed in this atmosphere turn out to be feasible during the reality testing period that is to follow.

Action Planning Generates Confidence and Motivating Power in an Organization

I have found that, although relatively few people seem to use action planning, almost everyone can understand a good action plan when it is completed. And I am now convinced that any person, corporation, or team venture can increase productivity and significantly cut the chances of wasted effort by making use of clear goals and action plans. Goal-setting and action-planning demand a lot of work, but it now seems obvious to me that people who are going to be a part of the implementation of goals can accept them much better if they are presented with a well-thought-out plan.

Such a plan, by creating a sense of security and trust, cuts down on the ever-present fear of failure that lurks up and down corporate halls. And feelings of assurance are powerful motivators among employees. It is my strong suggestion that, except on very rare occasions, when the goals of a corporation or group are presented, they should always be accompanied by a plan for their accomplishment.

I'm presenting here an ideal model. It may not work completely for everyone, and will of course have to be modified to fit individual situations. But I think it will serve to illustrate the principle of action planning, which I find to be absolutely essential to accomplishing significant things. The incredible thing to me is that, by setting goals and designing action plans, I can understand every deal I go into with a depth I wouldn't have dreamed possible. This has taken a lot of the uncertainty and fear of failure out of my life.

But action planning alone isn't enough to ensure the success of a project. Even the best action plan must be checked and tested in the world of action. The process of checking will be the subject of the next chapter.

Chapter 13

CHECKING AND COMPLETING YOUR PLANS

After the overall action plans and the connecting links between different subgoals have been set up, the process of checking *each part* for feasibility begins. This is accomplished by going through each action plan, step by step, and checking until you feel that every step will work as you have planned it.

If you are examining a vocational change as a goal or thinking about starting your own business, you may have to do all the feasibility checking yourself. This can be done by getting the help you need from members of the profession you are considering or calling on such people as bankers, attorneys, and tax consultants for advice.

But if you are working in a corporate or group situation, now is the time to make full use of the expertise and experience of those on your team. (Even in corporate venturing, the initial dreaming and much of the overall action-planning has usually been done by the entrepreneur alone. The members of the team can help with working out the detailed plans or their own individual plans for specific smaller goals, and the ultimate review and checking occurs with the team—but only after the original plan has been mapped out.)

At this point, it is wise to *seek* criticism and alternate ideas. It may be that others can come up with better routes for reaching your goals than have been planned. In fact, it will probably be necessary to make modifications on most plans because of problems that are discovered in the checking process. But there's nothing wrong with adjusting the original plans; one of the main ingredients for success at this stage of the process is flexibility.

The electric atmosphere of holding to the basic goals while having to adjust both short-term targets and methods of reaching them is not an easy environment for some creative people to work in. This process requires someone who can keep a clear head while taking criticism and making substantial changes, if needed, in his or her own plans.

But it is better to do the adjusting now than later. Too many changes made *after* the plans have been finalized and a commitment has been made may demoralize the team members. The original action-planning and checking should be done so carefully that a minimum number of changes will have to be made after the startup.

The Problem of Egotistical Pride

If, in the process of checking, it becomes apparent that part of a plan won't work, there is a tendency in some people on teams to want to dismiss the whole plan. They may become very negative and critical and want to move on to other matters. When this happens, it's hard to keep from getting angry and discouraged, because a great deal of time and effort may have been put into developing the plan.

But this is one of those times which can separate those who succeed from those who fail. And often the crucial question is: will you go for help? When everyone on your team is stumped about a problem in your action plan and starts getting negative, don't give up. Go outside your organization and find some experts in the particular field in which the blockage showed up. Ask them to give their opinions about the particular point in question. (Don't hesitate to spend the money if you believe in your dream.)

Actually, asking for help is not particularly easy for me to do, and I suspect a lot of other people feel the same way. Pride can very easily get in the way of admitting I can't handle everything myself. But if you want to succeed in creative projects, particularly large ones, in this time of intense specialization, I believe you *must* be willing to admit what you don't know. Every week there are new, more efficient ways of handling difficulties in different fields. And since few people are able to keep up with the new thinking and discoveries outside their own specialty area, getting good help with problems is an absolute necessity. (I'll discuss this more in the chapter on experience.)

If the outside experts can't find a solution to a problem that has cropped up in an action plan, and you and your team can't find a way to work around the problem, simply admit that the action plan isn't feasible and move on to other plans—or other goals (if this plan was crucial to achieving the primary goal). This is also very difficult to do. Because of pride, I hate to admit a plan I have worked hard to develop just isn't going to work. But again, it is much better to discover this during an action plan check than after a commitment to invest a lot of time and money has been made.

Pride can sometimes be so intense that an entrepreneur or manager will insist on committing to a deal before anything like an action plan check has been made. There is a kind of irrational macho feeling of "Don't you have the guts to commit? Anyone can see this is a good deal."

One of the difficulties in our culture is that we are often taught that we must make our serious commitments "on faith"—the assumption being that one must commit first and find out the cost later. But even Jesus Christ was very insistent that before going into any serious commitments a person should *"count the cost"* in every way (Luke 14:28, RSV). And the shores (of both the religious and business worlds) are littered with the shipwrecks of those who in their enthusiasm and egotistical pride did not bother to even check the feasibility of what it was they were committing to do and be.

So reserve the "go or no go" commitment decision for a later date, and check until you are completely satisfied, even if your team gets restless or negative.

Why It's Important to Check

It may seem that I'm spending an unusual amount of time on the process of planning, checking and reshaping plans. But in some ways this is the key area which can determine whether or not the startup of a business or other creative venture will be a positive and exciting experience or a horror chamber of bad surprises, strained relationships, and anxious, stressful days and nights. Also, I have found that any extended time I spend on designing and checking action plans before making a commitment is more than made up for later by time saved because of the relative absence of unforeseen problems.

Even with the perfect action plan, totally checked out, there will have to be changes, because the conditions in the world around you will be changing from the moment the plan is completed. But a good overall plan which has been thoroughly checked will allow you the freedom to address specific breakdowns after the commitment and startup without a general panic. And you will also be more free to spot *new* opportunities along the way toward your goals.

New Opportunities Call for New Goals and Plans

The true entrepreneur in any field knows that, "if things go" after he has set sail with his project, new and larger goals relating to the project may become visible on the horizon—goals which could not have been seen from the shore. And when this happens, the process of examining the new opportunity, setting goals, and making action plans should be repeated, with regard to the new and larger goals. The temptation is to adjust only the *goals* and go after the new ones. But remember, the people on your team are working on the basis of the *old action plans*, and the failure to go through the process again and adjust the original plans can cause the new opportunity to become the occassion for the failure to reach *either* the old or the new goals.

You may recall that at BFI in 1966, our initial goal was to become the largest waste-disposal company in the city of Houston. Our original action plan provided for expansion into two additional cities, if all went well in Houston.

As I mentioned, it was in the process of traveling around the country to develop our game plan for moving into those next two cities that I saw the timing opportunity for a much larger business venture. I came back and prepared a *new action plan* based upon the *new goal.* At first the goal—to become a large national company with operations in literally dozens of cities—appeared impossible. But as our action plans unfolded, we saw we could do this by developing a carefully designed system for acquiring other solid-waste companies that were already operating in cities across America.

This expansion opportunity, which led to the acquisition and development of Browning-Ferris, shows how goals can change as an enterprise grows. It also is an example of the principle (and advantage) of developing an action plan before entertaining negative considerations.

At the time of our deciding on the goal of becoming a large national company, we had only one million dollars in sales and no publicly traded stock. In looking back I realize that, if we had allowed ourselves to dwell on the reasons we could not grow to a company with over $550 million in sales, we would have shaken our heads, laughed (or cried) and gone back to collecting garbage. Instead, when we recognized the larger opportunity, we dreamed and looked at the needs of the owners of other companies. We isolated major and minor goals and did our figuring with calculators and computers. Then we spun a web of action plans, checked them, and tied them together within our final goal of becoming a national company.

Our creativity was bubbling over in all directions, because we had paper successes and no failure as we developed our secret action plans. But we would have faltered within days if we hadn't had a new action plan to go with the new goal.

You Don't Always Follow the Rules!

It is probably obvious by now that I believe the procedures involved in setting concrete goals and devising specific action plans to meet them is the matrix from which success comes in any creative effort.

Having said all this, however, I must confess that sometimes I have cut out whole steps in the planning procedure described here. I have made quick decisions without a plan when I have had enough information and experience to feel secure—even though the details were not worked out until later. Sometimes, on rare occasions, an opportunity of such obvious potential comes along that, after a brief investigation, a commitment seems justified.

When Keith Miller was in the oil exploration business, a major company official called him on a Tuesday morning, saying the company had just that day discovered that one of their leases was going to expire on Thursday of the same week if a well were not commenced on it.

A well on the adjacent property was currently producing a lot of natural gas. The geology indicated that a well drilled on the tract on which the lease was expiring had an *excellent* chance of being a producing well also. All of the company's rigs were tied up, and the only way to save the lease was to "farm it out." The official wanted to know if Keith's group would like to take the lease and start drilling operations before midnight on Thursday.

Keith knew the area and the company official and could check the geology and titles in a few hours. So, after locating a rig and arranging for the money, he committed to move onto the location and commence drilling a nine-thousand-foot gas well within forty hours. Ordinarily, getting a deal that size together would take a good bit more time and planning. But in this case, because of the circumstance, a rush commitment seemed justified.

The Finished Plan

"Emergency" opportunities, like the one described above, are exceptions rather than the rule. In the vast majority of cases involving creative ventures, it is very important to take the time to work out an action plan and check it carefully. As I have suggested, the total detailed plan will be a blueprint for the operation, as well as a careful management plan for coordinating the smaller specific tasks which fit logically together. It will serve as a constant reference map by which the instigator or manager can observe breakdowns and slowdowns and help everyone stay on the right track.

After the decision is finally made to go ahead with the project, an intense discipline will be needed to focus on one thing only—reaching the overall goal through the action plans that have painstakingly been set! But remember, that decision to go has not yet been made. Before we consider the decision itself, I think it might be good to stop and take a look at the roles of capital and experience—two crucial factors in the success of any action plan.

Chapter 14

THE ROLE OF CAPITAL

Capital is "the total amount of money or property owned or used by an individual or corporation." * But I would like to suggest that for the purposes of this discussion we separate personal expenses, houses, and cars from the category of capital and think of capital as money supplied by the owners to make a business (or other venture) go.

If your creative dream does not require this sort of investment capital you may want to skip this chapter. I am assuming that the reader who continues here is interested in questions concerning the capital which is necessary for creative commercial ventures.

"Adequate" Capitalization

How much invested capital does a venture need, and how much should be borrowed to start operating? It's at the point of "adequate capitalization" that my own philosophy seems to contrast most sharply with the popular notion of the way an entrepreneur operates. There are hundreds of stories of very successful people who have made a great deal of money by an aggressive use of enormous financial leverage—that is, they have *invested* a very small percentage of capital and *borrowed* a large percentage of the money needed for their business. For example, a friend of mine in Houston has become one

* *Funk & Wagnalls Standard Desk Dictionary*, s. v. "capital"

of the largest real estate developers in the world through the use of financial leverage.

But my own preference is to be much more cautious. I try to get a *large* percentage of the money needed to start the business through capital investment, and to borrow as *little* as possible. I prefer to be aggressive in the areas of *planning, operation,* and *development,* while maintaining a very conservative attitude toward capitalization.

This preference is not based on a whim, but on the fact that I have been examining companies carefully over the years and have been personally involved in the development of several. I feel sure that my father's painful experience with being undercapitalized has influenced me deeply. But I have also seen that the highway to success is strewn with the crumpled bodies of otherwise creative ventures in which the owner or manager tried to do too much with too little money and saw his dreams shrivel and die.

Under the best conditions determining the "amount of capital necessary" is a very difficult decision. And it is very easy to underestimate what is really going to be required.

When estimating the amount of capital needed, many people overlook several factors; this can cause the estimates to be very unrealistic. Two of these factors involve egotistical pride and can be compensated for.

The Human Factor

In the exhilaration of starting a creative enterprise, it is easy to forget the "human factor" in the equation. Even if the goals are clear and the action plans are complete and checked, human beings will be developing and staffing the business. And we human beings seem to have a strange blindness to the fact that we make *many* mistakes in our calculations, our decisions, and our performances. And unless the underlying capital foundation allows for some *pretty significant mistakes* in planning, judgment, and execution, a business which appears on paper to have adequate capitalization may be seriously undercapitalized.

I have come very close to disaster myself by making financial plans that didn't allow for any serious mistakes. For example, when I started the first garbage company and did my figuring on the basis of ninety days' advance billings, there was no room for the miscalculations about the capacity of our first truck. And we almost went under because of my bad judgment.

Personally, I *always* want to have enough "extra" capital to keep things going without panic while any possible major operational or management problem is being solved.

Estimating Performance and Profit

By the time one has gone through dreaming, recognizing an opportunity, setting goals, and making action plans for a new venture, he or she is usually so excited and enthusiastic that *any* estimates concerning performance and/or profits may be a little suspect. And the normal inertia (because of newness) which must be overcome in the beginning often makes for an even lower-than-estimated performance.

Regardless of how good a new business looks, I never expect it to make a profit right away. So I think in terms of providing enough capital to make it through the first period of operation without much income. What has worked for me in determining the amount of capital needed is to take my most conservative projection of the income we can generate through our efforts in the business, and then discount that by 20 to 40 percent. I am generally a very positive thinker, but I am a realist—almost a pessimist—in this area of performance.

This formula—requiring that capital investment provide the 20 to 40 percent "extra"—may seem unrealistic, but if a person doesn't provide adequate capital for the beginning of a venture, that venture may become one of the 95 percent of new businesses which fail before the end of the second year. Financial reality is very hard to face, but, hard as it is, it's easier at the planning stage than later, after a serious commitment has been made.

In my own experience, the philosophy of allowing a "cushion" in providing capital has worked very well. Generally, the companies I have been involved in building have really needed the additional capital in order to take advantage of new opportunities in the industry or to compensate for mistakes and setbacks. For example, when Browning-Ferris took over a large bankrupt company in a Southeastern city and unexpectedly lost a lot of money, the several hundreds of thousands of dollars in "extra" capital we had provided kept a lot of lumps out of our throats.

Effects of Undercapitalization

The effects of undercapitalization are often not clearly understood by a young businessperson. Capital, being the lifeblood of any business, is directly related to its *ongoing* creative health and to its growth potential. When, through errors in planning or execution, it is discovered that the capital is not adequate, a wave of panic can come over you. There are suddenly intense pressures and stresses—both on interior operations and on financial relations with customers, suppliers, and banks.

This stress can affect your performance and the performance of the people around you, causing additional costly errors in judgment. Suddenly you are in the position of frantically putting out financial fires in the hold while trying to steer the boat. This is not to mention the ill-will and deterioration of credibility which can develop from late payment of bills and other obligations. In addition, the fear of failure which can accompany the sudden awareness of being undercapitalized is liable to severely affect morale within your company—all because the human factor and the tendency to be overoptimistic were ignored when developing capital strategy.

Financial Gunslingers

The history of the business world—especially in the United States—is full of flashy financial gunslingers who ride fast and hard with their business ventures, depending on charm and manipulative tactics in order to "beg, borrow, or steal" the capital they need "on the trail."

But besides being an extremely self-centered approach, this

is a dangerous way to treat one's investors and business associates. One false step, and the venture can fail. When this happens, the reputations and happiness of all the people on the team can be destroyed or tarnished.

In addition, the gunslinger attitude can put the well-being of the entrepreneur's entire family in constant jeopardy and poison the very atmosphere in which they must live and grow together.

Besides, a significant failure in a business or other vocation, and the consequent loss of face, can have crippling emotional side effects. A man or woman with a serious vocational failure on his or her record may in turn feel like a personal failure. And even though this may not be true, the loneliness and sadness of such an experience can take the subtle edge off the magic creative confidence which characterizes a genuine entrepreneur.

With these things in mind, it seems almost inexcusable to endanger a venture or one's personal happiness by taking a careless attitude toward capitalization.

An Example

I once counseled with a young doctor, right out of medical school, who had just established his practice. This young man, whom I'll call Burt, had carried forward debts from his education and the cost of equipment for his office. But within a few months he had all the patients he could handle and was making a very good living.

A banker told Burt that he was considered to be a real winner. And because of the bank's confidence in him, it was prepared to lend him up to $150 thousand dollars. Burt was elated. He came to me for advice, saying that he felt a responsibility to use that money for investments.

I told him that, if I were he, I'd wait until I had my debts cleared up before making any financial investments.

But then a man named Morton came along and offered Burt a piece of a real estate development deal. Mr. Morton was very persuasive and, without doing any checking, Burt borrowed twenty-five thousand dollars and entered the deal.

In a few months, Morton came back. He said, "Everything's going great Burt, better than we'd hoped—but in order to make the deal work the way it should, we'll need another twenty-five thousand." Six months later, Morton came back, and an additional twenty-five thousand was invested the same way.

Burt was getting a little nervous, but Morton kept assuring him that the deal was solid—it was just costing more "because it's turning out to be a bigger deal than we'd thought." Nine months later, Morton came back to see Burt. This time he wore a serious face and said, in effect, "This deal will still go, but we've hit a crisis point. If you don't invest another fifty thousand, you'll lose all you've put in."

At this point Burt came to me for advice with a very pale face and anxious look in his eyes. After we talked it over and he'd explained the way the project had developed, I advised him not to invest any more money in the deal. But the fear of losing the whole seventy-five thousand he had invested drove him to borrow the additional fifty thousand.

The sad ending to the story is that Burt ended up losing the whole $125 thousand. During the next few years he had to devote all of his efforts and income toward repaying that money, plus interest. His wife was unhappy because she and their children couldn't have the things other doctor's families had, and their relationship soured. Burt became bitter and cynical and eventually left the practice of medicine. While he'd been good at his profession, he didn't have a sound philosophy about the use of capital, and he ruined his vocation—and perhaps his life.

Big Ventures Need Adequate Capital, Too!

Now, you may feel that my conservative approach is unreasonable for you because you are unable to get "adequate" capital for the size project you have in mind. But if, after extensive investigation, you find that the American financial system will not provide the amount of capital necessary, you may have to face the fact that the probable success of the project is at least questionable. In the exciting presence of what seems to be a really big idea, a stimulated ego can often whisper to you, "*you* can do it—even if they won't come up with all the money you asked for!" But watch out. The *size* of the project is not usually the deterrent in getting capital, in any case. And the need for adequate capital is even greater in a long and difficult venture.

For example, a sane person might consider a very short trip across the desert without taking adequate water. But it does not follow that, on a much longer trip, he or she will find it somehow *easier* to manage without enough water. Undersupply is always dangerous.

How Large Do You Want to Grow?

In considering ambitious business ventures, I have found it very helpful to remember and follow a particular principle which pertains to obtaining capital: if one is building a large company, he or she can afford to wind up with a smaller percentage of ownership. Selling portions of the company can be a valuable source of capital while the business is expanding.

I am aware that many entrepreneurs would consider this approach outright heresy. But again I believe that it is essential to keep one's focus on the primary goal. If it is building a large company, one must be careful to move toward that goal in the most effective way possible, and not kill the dream by greed.

For example, in the early stages of BFI, after having been in the residential garbage collection business for about one year, we expanded into commercial collection with the purchase of a third truck. At that time, our estimates indicated that we needed twenty-five thousand dollars in the bank. This capital was raised by selling 20 percent of the company.

Months later, when we started in the disposal (in addition to the collecting) business, we put $110 thousand in the bank through the sale of an additional 20 percent of the company. And then a little later, in 1968, we made the decision to expand into two other cities with $700 thousand in the bank. The additional capital funds came through a private placement in which a new investor purchased another 20 percent of the company.

All of our commercial bankers said we had given up too large a share of the company. But our goal was to build the largest and best disposal company in the world. And we got the capital when we needed it, even though we wound up selling a large percentage of the ownership before we were through.

It seems to me that what happened at BFI is ample evidence that this principle can work. In 1968, when we began expanding, there were several companies with garbage operations a lot larger than ours. By the time our expansion was completed in 1973, there were none. And I believe that any success we experienced at BFI was in large measure due to our conservative attitude toward capitalization.

No Effective Universal Rules

But having said all this, I would hesitate to give any simple formulas for determining just how much capital a *particular* venture may require. When you have estimated how much money you will need overall, you will have to determine how much will be provided by invested capital and how much will be borrowed.

The ideal debt-to-assets ratio depends on many factors, such as: How liquid are your assets? How reliable is your cash flow? How fast will your inventory turn over? Even such things as the custom of the industry regarding the billing and payment of accounts receivable have an effect on the amount of capital that is needed. Since these factors will vary greatly, depending on the nature of the business, an individual decision has to be made for each new venture.

Also, there are factors related to the nature and place of the business in the public's esteem and confidence which allow for very different approaches to financial leverage. For example, commercial banks work on a system that involves enormous financial leverage—perhaps an eight to one debt to equity ratio. No industrial corporation would consider leverage to the extent these banks do. Yet I do not believe there is reason for undue alarm about the existing banking system. There are well-tried policies which make the system work.

Each business occupies a unique position in relation to the business community at large, to the public, and to the financial institutions it must deal with. So it seems very unwise to state a specific capital strategy to apply to any new venture—especially until the goals and action plans for that venture have been carefully examined. Each individual case will have to be considered according to its own requirements.

You Can Get Help

In most areas in the United States, one can get good advice relating to proper capitalization for any size venture. Accountants, other businessmen, and bankers can help in the development of strategy. (And such people are also often helpful in giving counsel about financial needs relating to vocational changes.)

In summary, I'd just say that, before getting into a new business venture which requires a lot of money, I would get some expert advice from financial advisors familiar with the type business you are entering. After estimating my capital requirements as accurately as possible, I would add a percentage for the "human factor" and another for possible exaggerated sales or performance figures. *Then* I would make sure that I had experienced people to make every area of the business go well.

Chapter 15

GETTING THE "EXPERIENCE" YOU NEED

The elements we have already mentioned—deep desire, an ability to dream and to recognize significant opportunities, a sense of timing, specific goals, workable action plans, and adequate capital—all are essential to the process of creative enterprise. An enthusiastic and positive attitude which draws people into one's adventure is also very important. But unless the necessary experience is brought into the process at the planning stage, the odds are stacked against success for even the most talented innovator.

The Meaning of Experience

I am using the term "experience" to mean that particular kind of practical wisdom needed to accomplish a specific task efficiently—the wisdom which comes from having done the task successfully before. The first time a person tries to do something new—whether it is playing chess, riding a bicycle, or constructing a building—he or she will probably make a number of clumsy mistakes. This is simply because each endeavor has its own peculiar set of "rules" or principles which must be learned before the activity can be done well.

I remember when I first went skiing. I had a hard time getting it through my head that in skiing—unlike other sports I'd known—I needed to keep my weight forward instead of back.

It also seemed unrealistic to lean *downhill* in order to *slow down*. But I soon found that unless I wanted to eat a great deal of snow and risk some broken bones, these principles had better be learned and followed.

A person who is just learning to ski must focus his or her primary effort on staying upright and learning how to change direction. But a more experienced skier can concentrate on where he or she wants to go and approach troubled areas without panic, because the "how to"s have become second nature. Experienced skiers don't have to waste time and energy trying to keep their balance in a complicated situation; they can make the sharp turns to avoid unexpected rocks or crevices quickly and easily.

There are analogies to this in pursuing most creative ventures. For example, in the real estate business, an experienced attorney who has examined the titles to lands in a certain county can often examine an abstract of a title in that area and give an opinion in a fraction of the time it might take an inexperienced attorney. The experienced attorney (or builder or physician), like the experienced skier, can often save a great deal of time and energy and can handle unexpected problems in a natural and efficient way. And since time, labor, and the handling of unexpected problems are crucial elements in the success of all kinds of ventures, experience in a given field is a very important element to check when drawing up an action plan.

Few of us have all the experience we need to accomplish our really important goals. When we are plotting a new direction in life or planning a large project, there will be many problems and areas of expertise we will have to deal with simultaneously—and some we will know very little about.

It seems obvious that the answer is to seek help from those who do have the necessary expertise and experience. But there is sometimes a strange difficulty at this point, because many of us tend to let a particularly stubborn kind of pride stand in the way of seeking the help we need.

It's Hard to Admit We Need Help

For some peculiar reason, many of us—particularly men—have been indoctrinated with the subtle conviction that to ask for help of any kind is a weakness. We are led to believe that we should be able to do things ourselves—at least by the time we are grown. Such an attitude makes it difficult for us to ask for help, even when we need it desperately. Sometimes this stubborn independent streak makes it difficult for me to receive love and valuable suggestions even from my own family—maybe especially from my own family.

False pride, the tendency to resist going for help or receiving it, can take on tragic proportions. A long-time friend, the vice president of a large company and a man in the prime of life, was required by company policy to have a free annual physical at the Mayo Clinic, but he would not go. He smoked a lot and had a bad cough, but he just laughed and ignored his family when they urged him to get a check-up.

Finally, after a couple of years, the cough got so bad that he had to go to the doctor—but it was too late. A few months later he was dead of lung cancer, probably because he would not let himself go get help.

The ability to face one's limitations seems to be one of the key marks of maturity. For example, little children don't have any understanding of their own mortality; in the childish mind there is an ego-blind and naive sense that "I will live forever" and that "I can handle it" without regard to the seriousness of the situation. This is also what makes adolescents, who have received the strength of adulthood without the knowledge of their own limitations, do some bizarre and sometimes fatal things.

As strange and tragic as it may seem, many innovators of all kinds, entrepreneurs, and managers have a similar childish attitude toward getting experienced help in reaching their goals. In the face of all reason, they brush off suggestions of getting help, saying, "Don't worry—*I* can handle it!"

I know a man who once was one of the most successful

real estate brokers in Texas. He made a great deal of money and invested it, using a lot of financial leverage. When the interest rates caused a slowdown in the trading of real estate, this man was caught with huge investment payments due and a greatly reduced income.

If he had gone to his creditors for help, it is likely he could have salvaged much of what he had. But he wouldn't take any advice; he tried to bluff his way through the bad time alone, assuming conditions would change. Because of his pride, this man has lost most of what he had accumulated, plus the respect of many people whose payments he ignored.

In many ways pride can be the most serious block to lasting success in any creative enterprise. A person who is serious about pursuing a dream will learn to recognize the limitations of his or her own knowledge, will put aside pride and go after the experience needed to successfully complete the project.

Build Experience into Your Plans

I am suggesting that, when you have set the goals for a venture and are developing the action plans, you should carefully consider the need for experience. Examine every necessary step in which you lack experience, to see whether someone could be brought in to plan or check out the task efficiently. (Of course, how much "experience" it will take to accomplish a given set of goals will depend on whether they involve working alone or as part of an organizational team. But I believe the principles are similar in either case.)

In implementing any creative dream, you should also make provision, as part of the action plan, to bring in experienced people after the startup of the venture. They can assume responsibility for any areas of the operation not covered by adequate experience. If it is not possible to bring in the experienced people you need, you may be able to get training yourself or send some members of your team to get trained before you actually begin.

Bringing in experienced people on your team may not be as easy as it sounds. It can be threatening to any innovator or entrepreneur to have, in his or her organization, people who may have more knowledge and experience than he or she does. But if the entrepreneur really wants to achieve clearly stated goals, he or she will do well to try to overcome pride and the fear of being thought inadequate. The acquiring of the necessary experience can go a long way toward avoiding failure and achieving faster, longer-lasting success.

An Example of Getting Experience

In 1968, when we at BFI recognized the opportunity to build a national company, we devised an action plan and set out under my leadership to build the company. But, as I stated earlier, nothing happened—for twelve months we had absolutely no success. Here (again) is what happened.

After brainstorming and trying every approach we could think of, we went for help—to Lou Waters at Underwood, Neuhaus. Through consultation he showed us what our difficulties were and helped us see how to proceed.

This encounter with Lou helped me realize that we needed to bring into our organization experienced help with major financial planning and execution. I simply didn't have the necessary experience at the financial level we were moving into. So we finally convinced Lou to come with BFI. And since in our organization there was no place for a person of Lou's stature except at the top, he was brought in as chairman of the company. It seemed strange to ask someone to come in at that level, but we needed his experience to accomplish the very large goals we had set for ourselves.

As our momentum picked up and our action plan unfolded, we saw that the companies we were acquiring had a variety of internal management styles and different levels of management expertise and efficiency. That was when we asked Harry Phillips to join BFI as president.

At that point, BFI really took off in terms of new acquisitions, operational efficiency, coordination of all efforts, and marketplace success. And there is no question that the reason for the speed and relative ease with which well over one hundred companies were acquired and integrated into one was that, in every major area of our expansion, we had enormously capable and experienced people.

The Cost of Experience

Getting the experience that is necessary to make any creative venture go can be costly. For me it meant recruiting someone else to be chairman and president of a company I had started, loved, and felt an important part of. Yet, because I had set definite goals, I was aware of a very important fact. There was no way to take advantage of the opportunity which existed in the garbage industry at that time, and thus meet my goals, without strong, experienced people like Lou Waters and Harry Phillips.

I realize this raises an obvious question concerning what the innovator or entrepreneur gets from the venture. If one isn't the publicly acknowledged leader, "what's in it" for him or her? This is such an extremely important point that I think it's worth a serious look.

Another Way to Win

Some people seem to have an inborn need to try to be number one. But, although the need is widely experienced and admired, the *expression* of this need is not considered to be in good taste in a society based on Judeo-Christian ideals. So we go along through life feeling the need to be in the big winner's circle, but refusing to express it or admit it even to ourselves.

As a young man I had a deep yearning to be a winner. As I've mentioned, I was interested in sports, and I had accumulated certain small awards in high school—like being class president and captain of the football team. These encouraging signs fed my inner hope that someday I might be number one in some important effort.

But at Rice University a paralyzing kind of fear gripped me. I wasn't good enough to become a big star in football or make outstanding grades. These are not unusual discoveries for a small-town boy going to a sophisticated university, but they were new and very disturbing to me. Was I going to make it in life—or even at school?

During the next months and years I began to undergo some changes. And gradually, although I don't remember when, I became aware of several truths about human nature and "being number one." These insights led me to discover what is perhaps the greatest source of human power available to get things done toward the accomplishment of creative dreams.

First, I realized that, clustered near the top of each field of endeavor, there are dozens of star performers, people who have paid their dues and are ready to take the final step into the winner's circle. But I also saw that there is an interesting dynamic involved here. Being known as *first* is the thing; one does his job with great desire and even meets other people's goals in order to climb toward being first. But these other goals are often being accomplished in one sense, "along the way." This means, for example, that a star quarterback will often help a coach fulfill his dream of having a winning team. And at the same time the coach gives the quarterback the opportunity to fulfill his own dreams of being the best in the conference.

I also realized, during those long months of trying to survive as a student—feeling very much over my head academically and like a failure as an athlete—that I would probably never be able to be number-one in the world as an individual performer. This realization was a devastating blow, but it eventually led to a whole new way of thinking.

A little later, while I was working to build Browning-Ferris, it occurred to me that, if I were willing to let other people be the publicly acknowledged leaders, I might then be able to put together a team of number-one performers. And in the process we would stand a much better chance of building a very outstanding company that would achieve our largest goals. My satisfaction would come in knowing I'd caused it to happen—and of course in having a few friends whom I respected know it too. I marvelled at the simplicity of this approach and remembered someone years before saying, "You can accomplish almost anything with a talented group if you don't care who gets the credit."

Sharing the Credit Really Works!

Once I really grasped the implications of this approach, it was much easier to go for and get the best people to join BFI when the time came. At the same time, I was making it possible for them to fulfill their individual dreams, as together we accomplished our larger corporate goals.

In addition to bringing in top people to *head* the company, we attempted to recruit the very best men and women we could find for *every* part of our business.

I can see that the policy of seeking out people with quality experience and helping them fulfill their dreams might work wonders in sales organizations, and particularly in political or religious institutions. Imagine a church in which the professional minister sought out the best laypeople he could find, giving them a place to preach, teach, or fulfill their dreams of serving God in all kinds of creative ways. What if the minister let *them* get the credit for what happened through their work, and he took a low profile position himself. He could dream, set goals, and do action plans with parishioners for creative things they might do together for God and for other people. The results might be surprising.

Some Advantages of This Approach

When a gifted person is given a place to fulfill his or her dreams with freedom and stature, the creative energy released is more than I could have imagined.

In addition, there are several side benefits to be found in this style of leadership. An innovator who surrounds himself or herself with the most talented people in the field learns the total enterprise more thoroughly and quickly—and with fewer mistakes and failures—than would be possible any other way. And at BFI we found that the more experienced people we had the less the fear of failure bothered us.

We also found that having a depth of experience helped us in other concrete ways. We discovered, for instance, that financial institutions often make the decision to lend to one developer over another on the basis of their confidence in the developer's experience. Even though the same market conditions and the opportunity to employ the same contractors and architects exist, the loans are typically—and for good reason—made to the developers with experience. This principle seems to apply equally well in virtually all aspects of life. For instance, research grants, institutional approval for new ideas in a department of a corporation, or proposals for social or religious action projects are often judged and supported (or rejected) on the basis of whether or not quality experienced people are involved.

Finally, besides all the material and psychological advantages of having highly experienced people on the team, the entrepreneur receives a very personal benefit. There is something esthetically beautiful about watching a quality person with great experience perform a task—whether it is a star running back, a world-class skier, a brilliant preacher, or a skilled construction contractor.

Get the Experience You Need

I realize that this brief discussion is simplistic when it comes to the complexity and speed of modern creative venturing. I also know that in some cases it is just not possible to get all the experienced people you would like to. But whatever the field, I am convinced that getting the proper experience or training is very important to success. The savings in time, energy, and costly mistakes makes possible the fulfillment of large—and small—dreams which otherwise could never have gotten off the drawing board.

Chapter 16

THE FINAL DECISION—NO RECONSIDERATION

There are some very successful business and professional people who apparently go into new projects with an almost casual attitude of "Hey, this is a good idea." They seem to treat the venture as a sort of cross between a hobby and a trip to Las Vegas. But while I don't think one should go into even a very significant enterprise with a grim countenance, I do think that committing to a really substantial venture is a very serious matter. Such a commitment can be a real watershed moment—if you understand what's really involved.

The decision to commit will affect your whole life, and that of your family, perhaps for many years to come. The *depth* of commitment necessary to accomplish a large goal is one reason I have put off a discussion of the decision until we have looked at some reasonable checking procedures.

I do not believe that the kind of commitment it takes to accomplish really significant goals is for everyone. Many people are already content with their lives and have no desire to commit the enormous amount of creative energy it takes to accomplish a large new vocational goal. Perhaps such an intense commitment is only for a very few. But even if one is not considering a large life-changing goal I believe many of the principles addressed in this chapter will apply to anyone facing an important commitment of any kind—especially a vocational commitment.

The Process to This Point

In preparing for the point of commitment, you will have felt the strong desire, which has grown as you have examined the opportunity. You will have prepared yourself properly by choosing the right (timing) moment, setting specific goals, and designing careful action plans. And you will have addressed the areas of capital and experience. Only after you have done these things has the time come to make the decision concerning whether or not to commit to achieve the goals.

As the earlier chapters indicate, by this time you may have spent a sizeable amount of time and money investigating the opportunity—setting goals and preparing action plans. But *don't ever* let that push you into committing a great deal *more* time and money to a deal unless you are truly enthusiastic about giving yourself to it.

In any case, let's assume you have "walked through" the building of a new business and checked all the areas mentioned here. You have resolved any other questions which may have come to mind. Now, you are ready to step back, look at the overall dream with its goals and challenges, and make a decision.

The Moment of Truth—No Turning Back

The moment of truth has arrived. I would advise taking plenty of time in making this decision. Examine all the alternatives. Ask yourself: "Can I accomplish my life goals any other way?" "Is there anyone I haven't asked whose advice would give me a better perspective on this venture?" "Am I willing to exclude other major projects—even good ones—which may come along while I am completing this one?"

(Sometimes at this point the people who are close to you can exert a profound influence one way or the other. For instance, as I was deciding whether or not to go into the garbage business, I had a tremendous amount of encouragement from my father to move forward—though almost everyone else thought it was a crazy idea. My father even decided to go in with me on the project. His willingness to put his own time and effort into the business had a substantial influence in helping me decide to go ahead.)

I recommend this sort of careful thought because I believe that making the decision to move forward in any major project should be like Lindbergh's taking off across the Atlantic—there is *no turning back* in the middle of the ocean.

My friend Roger Ramsey, who was chief financial officer at Browning-Ferris during our rapid expansion, had very strong feelings about this attitude. After a certain commitment had been made by the company, I remember his telling another member of the management team, "Listen, failure isn't even an option from here on in!"

Of course, I am aware that circumstances can change drastically, and that sometimes it becomes obvious that you must get out of a deal fast to keep from pouring good money after bad (e.g., when someone has cheated you or withheld necessary information). But here I am talking about an *attitude,* a commitment which is so strong that solutions to seemingly impossible problems can sometimes be found.

I repeat, *be extremely careful* about making this commitment decision, because to have the creative enterprise process work for you, as it is capable of doing, you must feel you will go to the "absolute ends of the earth" to succeed. Your integrity and honesty need never be compromised, but, other than that, *let nothing stop you.*

(Some people have rationalized and said that in order to make it today, it is necessary to cheat on taxes or important government rules and regulations. I do not believe that. If your action plan provides for all the regulations, you can make it and still obey the laws.)

As I reread what I have just written, I realize it sounds melodramatic, and could sound arrogant. But I do not mean it that way. It's just that the obstacles which must be faced and overcome in any really significant vocational venture—the negative opinions of enemies and associates, the unforeseen blocks to your plans, the fear of failure which can jump out from nowhere at any time—all of these things require the instigator to make a commitment which is so deep as to be virtually unshakable. Such an attitude is so rare in this time of tentative commitments, and yet it is so central to success in the creative enterprise process, that I can't emphasize it enough.

After the Decision

When you have made a decision of this type, you will probably feel a real sense of exhilaration in knowing that you are willing to go forward, regardless of the difficulties and disappointments that are bound to follow. It seems as if, in the excitement of a new venture and with all the preparation I've recommended, it would be easy to keep such a commitment. But for me that hasn't always been the case.

I have mentioned the time, during the early stages of building the garbage company in Houston, when I was juggling the garbage business, my accounting practice, and my friend's new business—all in the "tax season" of 1966. I got so physically and emotionally exhausted I could hardly think. And when it looked like the day-to-day problems and decisions were going to overwhelm me, I wanted with everything in me to quit and hang it up.

I was scared to death and sick of the whole deal. It was only as I thought about my life and about what was really important to me that I remembered my commitment to make it "no matter what." Then something deep inside finally told me to go on, and I did. But I was that close to quitting.

So I'm not saying it's easy to commit this way, or even that everyone who wants to reach his or her goals should make such a firm decision. But as I talk to people about their lives, and read biographies of men and women who've succeeded at what they set out to do, I become more and more convinced that the kind of all-out commitment I'm describing is a large part of what it takes to build a company, make a good marriage, or change a nation.

As a venture matures, you will be called on to make many additional commitments similar to the initial decision. Any time a new service line or product line is being considered, or a substantial expansion is on the horizon, all of the things I have described up to now—including the commitment decision—will need to take place again.

No Negative Attitude After the Decision

There was a time, in the early stages of BFI, when we were considering going into the "commercial" garbage business in Houston. We went through the careful process of goal-setting and agreeing on an action plan, which involved borrowing a considerable amount of money. We debated the negatives. Then, after we made the decision, the bank agreed to loan us the money.

As we walked out of the bank, one of the investors suddenly became very negative about the deal. As I have mentioned earlier, the time for criticism and questioning is *before* the decision is made. Once the commitment is made, you must move forward.

It immediately was obvious to me that that investor had to be taken out of the venture, because with his attitude he was going to continually be an impediment to the future success of the business. So we brought him out.

This may sound very severe, but it indicates how serious I am about keeping the commitment to succeed clearly in view. In several different ways I am saying that, once the decision to "go" is made, the total commitment of the innovator (aside from staying in close touch with God and family) must be directed at the success of the venture.

And this is not just true in business. Many of the people who have caused great development in the realms of art, politics, social concern, and religion have operated from a base of deep personal commitment to their goals. Some who come to mind are Vincent Van Gogh, Abraham Lincoln, Martin Luther King, and the Apostle Paul.

These people focused their lives so completely on their goals that, in spite of incredible odds against them, they were able to bring something important to their whole generation and beyond. It is out of this kind of commitment that a new ambiance can evolve within a family or an organization—an atmosphere in which the chances for success are greatly increased. And that atmosphere can lead to and reenforce a very powerful and positive attitude.

Chapter 17

THE IMPORTANCE OF ATTITUDE

Why do some creative people who have done their homework and made a serious commitment succeed against terrific odds, while others—equally gifted and in apparently similar circumstances—start out strong but then sag and fail to reach their goals?

I think one very crucial factor is attitude. Apparently most of us are aware of the necessity of having positive attitudes if we are to reach our goals, especially if we are in leadership positions. But for years I didn't realize the extent to which we can *determine* and *control* our attitudes.

The Power of Positive Thinking

About fifteen years ago I read a book by Norman Vincent Peale entitled *The Power of Positive Thinking.* In a way, I hesitate to bring that particular book into this discussion, because I am aware that some critics have labeled the book simplistic. Others have said that it doesn't take into consideration the very real "shadow side" of life. In my opinion, though, such criticisms miss the powerful and motivating essence of Peale's message.

It seems that there is an underlying principle related to keeping one's mind in good condition which is somehow near the center of the whole process of creative enterprise. And that principle pertains directly to the ongoing attitude of any creative person.

All of us, it seems, have either glaring or hidden weaknesses and shortcomings—and of course this includes me. But I have evidently been programed to feel that I *should* do "well" with my life—so well in fact that I have been disappointed with myself over and over ever since I was a young boy. On one hand this desire to "do well" has been a great motivator, and this motivation is very helpful during periods when things are going smoothly and I am riding a high tide of positive feeling. At such times I feel self-confident, and my desire to succeed draws me forward. But when the emotional tide shifts, and I find myself in a damp cold fog of uncertainty—what am I to do then?

Norman Peale helped me to realize that at such times we may be able to raise our performance level enormously by using a mental technique which provides us with something to focus on consciously during the times when the depressive fog blots out the emotional landscape.

Focusing on Images of Positive Results

We can seldom change our negative feelings by concentrating on them directly. In fact, when we try to fight them or to deny them to ourselves, we often give such feelings additional power. But there is a way we can "bypass" negative or "down" feelings and get on with creative living.

The human mind has a strong attraction to pictures or images. If we can picture clearly in our minds a result we want very much, we have a strong capability to move toward the achievement of that result. (That's why the dreaming process described in chapter 7 is so important.) So when negative feelings drop on me like a hot wet blanket, I have developed a way to deal with them, using this notion of the attracting power of images.

Although I can't directly attack and defeat the bad feelings, I *can* look beyond them to imagine the goals *as being already accomplished.* And as I keep these images or pictures of my completed goals before my eyes, I can usually get up and begin doing something specific to bring me closer to reaching the goals. It is amazing to me that I can operate on the strength of these positive images even on days when I don't feel enthusiastic about *ever* reaching my goals.

When I have worked like this for a day, two days, a week, keeping my eyes on the images of goals being accomplished, suddenly the "sun may come out" emotionally, and I *feel like* going on again. In the meantime, I have gotten a lot closer to my goals *and have maintained* a positive attitude in my *behavior* if not in my natural feelings.

It is almost like priming an old hand pump. The first few strokes don't bring any results. But when you put a little water in "artificially," the dry strokes are soon replaced by water flowing from deep within the earth. And during dry periods, when I have primed the pump emotionally through an act of the will (by envisioning accomplished goals and doing specific tasks to move toward them), the enthusiastic feelings are then likely to take over again. And when they do, enthusiasm can flow from deep within once more, where it's fresh, authentic, and contagious.

This creative use of positive images can open the way for significant changes in a person's performance.

An Example of Positive Imaging

As I am writing this, I remember an incident from the 1960s. A doctor in Houston had two sons who were running on the same high school track team. Both Bruce Cameron and his brother were sprinters, and each ran one leg of the 440-yard relay.

As it happened, the Cameron boys' Houston team qualified for the state track meet finals—but just barely. The state record at this time was 41.9 seconds, much faster than the Houston team had ever run. As a matter of fact, because of their recent performance, some people felt they should not even be in the state meet. But the Cameron brothers really set their hearts on winning that race.

According to the past, it really didn't seem physically possible for that team to run the 440 in 41.8 seconds. But for the entire week prior to the event these two brothers wrote on signs all over the walls of their home "41.8." And they visualized their anchorman crossing the finish line first.

When the Houston team qualified for the finals, their time was slower than any of the other eight teams that made the cut. As a matter of fact, Dr. Cameron heard people laughing in the stands about the fact that a team that inferior had even made the state finals.

But the seemingly impossible happened. The Houston team finished first in the Texas State High School Championship Meet with the record time of 41.8 seconds.

Now I certainly am not suggesting that attitude alone allowed those boys to break the state record. But could they possibly have run a 41.8 race without thinking the way they did? Although that's a question no one can answer with certainty, I have come to believe that, since they had never achieved that time before, their mental attitude and their actions during the entire week prior to the event transformed their performance drastically.

The Positive Power Released by Believing

But even if one has a very clear positive image to shoot for, it seems to be essential that he or she really *believe* the image can be reached. And often coming to believe that a goal can be achieved releases a new energy which helps bring about the achievement of the goal.

Some years ago, when I was growing up, there was an almost universal opinion that running a mile in four minutes or less was just not humanly possible. Since no one had ever before recorded a four-minute mile, most people thought that a performance limit in that event had been reached. But a young runner named Bannister believed the four-minute barrier could be broken. And in 1954 Roger Bannister ran a four-minute mile. People could hardly believe it. Then, within a very short time, many others ran faster than four-minute miles.

It seems that until we believe something is possible, we don't achieve it. But in this case, a positive attitude that a four-minute mile could be run freed hundreds of others to do what had never been thought possible before.

I realize it could appear that I am being very naive. Life is not a series of athletic events. Achieving goals in any aspect of life, including entrepreneurial ventures and vocational challenges, is a very complex enterprise. But I think there is a strong tendency to forget just *how much* a reality-oriented positive attitude can influence the successful overcoming of significant obstacles as we move toward the accomplishment of our goals.

Sabotaging a Positive Attitude by Concentrating on Negative Feelings

In the most ideal circumstances there are certain habits which can sabotage a positive attitude without one's even being aware of what's happening. For example, a debilitating habit many people have is that of saying negative and unduly critical things about other people (or about their own particular circumstances). When I catch myself doing this, I am very disappointed in myself; I feel as if I am copping out. In reality, cutting down other people or blaming my circumstances are covers for my own failure to maintain good relationships and performance. The end result of critical and negative attitudes and conversations is the debilitation of creative energy—the opposite effect from that of Peale's idea of filling the mind with positive images and attitudes.

When saying that "negative and critical comments" are inappropriate, I am not of course suggesting that you should avoid serious questions which must be considered; there are times when, in order to handle issues honestly, you must express negative or critical opinions. What I'm talking about is an overall attitude which always seems to look for and point out the negative elements of even the most positive circumstances.

For example, I have a friend who seems to spend 85 percent of his time complaining. His first greeting is the prelude to a litany of unhappy complaints, and this always makes me want to escape and not be involved with him. He is the last person I'd want to do business with on a regular basis.

Please don't misunderstand. I know there are people whose lives are oppressive and who have legitimate needs. But there is something about my friend's complaining which doesn't seem to speak of his needs. He seems to see himself as the only innocent victim in a world of cruel, stupid, and unfair people—even though he has wealth, privilege, and friends around him. He's what someone aptly called an "injustice collector."

I believe that if somehow we can *become aware* of the absolutely poisonous effect of such negative habits, it is possible to change them—just as it's possible to change our eating or drinking habits when it finally gets through to us that our present habit patterns are leading directly to an early death. In a sense, a discussion of this subject may seem to be a digression here. But the creative enterprise process can be severely stifled by the poisonous effects of a negative attitude—whether one is involved in a business, a scientific laboratory, a church, or even a marriage.

Besides, there is a sobering fact about looking for the frightening or negative elements in your environment: looking for bad things with the expectation of finding them often *causes* them to happen! A friend told me that when he first went skin diving in the Caribbean there were some sharks and baracudas in the area. The diving instructor pointed out to him that if he would simply go about his own business of enjoying the underwater beauty and be alert, he'd probably do fine. "The people who get in trouble," he said, "are usually the ones who are so tense about possible danger that they make frantic thrashing movements when they see a shark or barracuda. This can bring on the very attack they fear." If a swimmer is a quiet observer, swimming peacefully and positively, he will probably never face an attack under water. I think there is an analogy here about always looking for and accentuating the negative aspects of one's business or personal environment.

Of course, in spite of all our efforts to the contrary, there *will* be waves of negative feelings and periods of discouragement which will sweep over us. And they will sometimes come regardless of the way things are going.

Receiving Help in Down Times

Sometimes when I've been especially discouraged and couldn't seem to snap out of it, I have had to go to God and to other people for help. It's not comfortable for me to even talk about this, since I am generally opposed to "unloading feelings" on other people. But here, I am talking about a special kind of situation and relationship.

The situation is when I'm at my wit's end and have tried every way I know to remain positive and effective—and have failed. At times like these I feel stumped and exhausted. The relationship within which I feel safe to discuss such feelings is one in which I feel known, cared for, and respected as a person. I must feel that the other person will be able to hear me without judging me or trying to "straighten me out." Actually, often I don't even want "advice." I've just found that when I can share my discouraged or fearful thoughts and know I've been "heard" and understood, I usually feel a lot better. As a result of discussing my problems, I often have new insights, or at least don't feel so alone.

Some people can go to their wife or husband for this sort of conversation. For others it's a friend, attorney, therapist, or minister. It was years before I could feel free to do this kind of sharing of my feelings with anyone, and I'm still a little uneasy about it sometimes. But the help I have received in getting outside myself has been very significant in helping me back to a positive attitude.

Having said all this, I want to quickly add that I think one should be very careful in picking someone to talk to in this way. There are two things to consider. First, admitting discouraged and inadequate feelings may make you feel vulnerable, so be sure to pick someone you trust. Second, I'd suggest that you consider the other person's ability to handle your discouragement. You may have had the experience of feeling very good one day until some negative person dumped their garbage on you, and then had your own spirits take a nose dive. Since this sort of thing can leave people feeling awful, try to be sensitive when you choose someone to talk to.

Looking at the Big Picture

Besides sharing with trusted people, another thing which has been helpful to me during my "down" times is learning to look at my life from a broader perspective.

I have become increasingly aware that in the universe I am just a small and vulnerable person. I started out here as a helpless baby and in time will return to the earth as a few grains of dust. This awareness of the fragile nature of life and of the enormity of space has made me more consciously aware of the reality and importance of God in my experience. And I've turned toward him in my private life.

For me, this has been the beginning of a personal, inner relationship to God, with whom I can share any of my thoughts and feelings. I am convinced that the continued sense of support and help from God is a very important part of my own security and creative freedom. The reality of this security has helped me risk doing things which seem to exceed my apparent abilities, and to maintain a positive attitude much of the time. When I feel the sense of God's reality and presence, I am more confident that, whatever happens, God will be there on the other side of the failure or the success. He will help me find a sense of balance and get on with the next thing for my life. This faith in God is a deep and important part of my life, and it affects my attitude in a very positive way.

The Source of a Positive Attitude

Apparently no one knows the source of a positive attitude. Some people who appear to have everything anyone could wish for seem to be perenially negative, while others who are crippled and virtually helpless radiate a very positive attitude.

Out of the Second World War came many accounts of prisoners of war and others in concentration camps who were confined for years under almost unbearable conditions—with very little food to eat, almost no medical care, and little physical exercise. Some survived and some didn't.

Dr. Viktor Frankl, an Austrian psychiatrist who was interned in one of the concentration camps, noticed that the physically strong were not necessarily the ones who survived at all, that often the oldest and most emaciated prisoners would live and the strong, young ones would die. As he began to talk to people and get to know them, he found that the ones who survived were most often people who had some kind of hope concerning the world "back home," perhaps a love relationship or a vocational dream. Hope was the factor which gave them a positive attitude, which produced the endurance and brought out unbelievable courage and tenacity. When, by any chance these people got word that their hope was groundless (e.g., that the loved one had been killed or been unfaithful), death might follow almost at once—sometimes within a few days.* A further example of the effect of a lack of meaning can be seen in the person who, though never having been seriously ill, dies within a few weeks or months after retirement.

If hope and meaning are the sources of a positive attitude, then it seems to me that it is very important for us to have some hope or faith, the source of which lies far beyond the success or failure of our creative venture. That way, if things get rough or failure occurs, life will not have lost its meaning.

But whatever long-term meaning you find for your life beyond your creative venture—whether it is a relationship, a philosophy, or God, I am suggesting that it must be something which can provide you with a deep sense of inner security and hope. For I am convinced that these are the sources of a positive attitude which can transcend disappointment and the threat of failure.

---

* For a vivid account of the motivational power of hope and meaning, see *Man's Search for Meaning,* by Viktor Frankl (New York: Pocket Books, Inc., 1975).

Chapter 18

FACING ADVERSITY

The positive attitude we have been discussing comes from within ourselves—our inner environment. But the adversity we will be examining in this chapter has more to do with factors and events originating *outside* our immediate personal control.

I know of a young man who sold everything he had to buy a large old motel, the only one on a major highway leading into a city of sixty thousand people. The week after he closed the deal, a decision was announced to reroute that highway around the city, a mile *beyond* my friend's motel. And a large chain operation announced its plans to build a beautiful new motel at the point where the bypass left the old highway. All this, of course would soon leave my friend high and dry. He was, he said, "facing adversity." What attitude could he possibly have that would be constructive toward this adversity?

The Will to Win

In the chapter on desire I talked about a will to win, a fierce commitment to succeed, no matter what. And throughout this book so far I have emphasized that, once you have done your goal-setting and planning and have made a commitment, then it's possible to feel that there isn't anything that can happen which will stand in the way of moving forward, toward the completion of whatever you set out to accomplish.

But before getting back to my friend's dilemma, I want to

say I realize fully it is one thing to *talk about* things like this and to make fierce commitments, and quite another to *live them out* alone in the face of crushing blows from the surrounding environment. And it is equally difficult to maintain this attitude when we fall victim to our own miscalculations about people or projections.

Very early in my own business career I discovered that there is a deceptive quality about the way I feel in the face of a crushing blow to my plans. When I try to set things right and can't see how I'm going to be able to do it after the first twelve hours, I feel a black cloud of doubt rolling in from the horizon of my inner life. By the end of the first day, I am tempted to say "I'll *never* be able to solve *this* one!" But I have learned, when this happens, to stop and consciously acknowledge that tomorrow *I* will be different, even if the circumstances remain the same. Then, I may have a new perspective, and that can give me the opportunity to take another tack or at least be able to see the "wreckage" more clearly and investigate other possible courses of action.

It is a great relief to me to know that most creative ventures are not like sports events. Once the sun sets on an athletic contest, it's all over—someone has either won or lost. But in a business, for instance, if it is properly capitalized, there is usually the opportunity to win tomorrow. Given the right preparation and ingredients, I am increasingly convinced that relatively few people have to lose.

When Adversity Strikes

When adversity does occur, the first thing I have learned to do is to take a realistic look at what has happened. How much of my action plan has been destroyed? What goals are threatened or how apparently unreachable? If my plan is on paper, I may study it like I would an electric circuit diagram to see what has been shorted out. But the most important thing when confronted with adversity is to concentrate on what to do *next,* not on what has gone wrong. Too often people tend to assess blame, ask haunting questions about why something did or did not happen, or feel sorry for themselves and attempt to elicit sympathy from others. But this is not only wasted energy; it also creates a negative atmosphere, like a dense fog, in which you and your associates must attempt to put things back together.

So don't ever take time for disappointment about a mistake while you are facing adversity. Force those kinds of feelings to one side by beginning to look at positive courses of action. The focus at this point is to come up with *a definite plan* that will provide an alternative method of accomplishing a particular end and get the overall action plan back on track.

The way an innovator faces and overcomes adversity determines whether or not he or she will succeed in almost any enterprise. But this is especially true in really big ventures—since it is virtually impossible to avoid serious adversity in a large and complex operation of any kind. Psychologically, adversity often triggers the fear of failure in a very intense way. To avoid withdrawing into ultraconservative waters, it is important to charge right back in the face of adversity—as a race car driver after a serious accident often drives again in the very next race.

I realize, as I've suggested, that it is often impossible to control one's emotions by direct mental manipulation. But I have discovered that one can learn to act *in spite of* fears and disappointments. As a matter of fact, I believe a person *must* learn to do this, in order to be a successful innovator or entrepreneur.

Checking Alternative Courses With Your Team of Advisors

If I have developed a team as a part of my action planning, I do not face adversity alone. It is sometimes my tendency to want to be the hero and come up with the solution myself, but I do not believe an entrepreneur or manager of a large enterprise can afford that luxury. So, especially in times of adversity, after seeing that I don't know what to do, I try to lay the problem on the table before my team and draw creative insights from them.

Besides being an important step toward finding a solution to the problem, asking for their help gives them a tremendous feeling of importance and of being needed. In response to this feeling they may come up with creative ideas and ways to get the whole venture back on the track which wouldn't otherwise have been considered. Many great soldiers were commissioned in the field and started outstanding careers through finding solutions to dilemmas in the face of great adversity, when their superior officers were at their wits' end.

Belief in God

It is at times like this that a belief in God has been a great help to me in several ways. In the first place, I feel that, even if I fail totally, God will be there. And not only will he give me another chance in life; he will also *teach me* through everything that has happened. In fact, I've come to believe that the pain and difficulties I experience, through the mystery of faith, become a kind of wisdom that acts as "fertilizer" for the success of future ventures. I'm convinced that what we learn through adversity is very valuable—if it doesn't make us bitter.

This belief in God has also helped me to be aware that the responsibility for the "entire world" doesn't rest on my shoulders. Somehow when I was growing up I got the idea that I was responsible for "making things right" when the people around me were unhappy. And I'd feel guilty when I couldn't solve all the problems that came my way. But in trying to commit the outcome of my life to God, I realized how presumptuous that was. And this realization has helped me relax and concentrate on reaching my goals the best way I can.

Another way my belief and faith have helped me is by enabling me to step back occasionally and look at the importance of my current project or business venture from the perspective of a thousand years. When I can do this, my megalomania tends to subside a little, and I realize that I am just a person working to achieve my goals and earn my daily bread.

But don't misunderstand. This attitude is not in conflict with my commitment to move forward "no matter what." It's just a recognition of the fact that, simply because I'm a human being living in the real world, certain things will not work out perfectly for me. And when I don't have this broader perspective on life, which helps me not to take myself too seriously, then the chances are rather great that in the face of adversity I may choke and revert to some sort of unhealthy stress behavior.

A belief in God, then, has helped me to learn from my failures, have a more realistic appraisal of my abilities and responsibilities, and work hard under the pressure when things go wrong without taking myself too seriously. It is a foundation that helps me keep my feet on the ground as I face adversity.

An Approach to Adversity

From the agonizing moment the Coca-Cola bottles went careening off my truck and crashing onto the streets of Houston, I have known what it is like to face adversity. And I will never forget the sweaty palms and the knot in my chest that first day in the garbage business in Houston when I realized our truck was too small—and it was my fault! Yet it was through experiences like these that I began to learn about the creative power which can be generated through the positive facing of adversity.

Later, at BFI, a positive, aggressive posture toward adversity was a common attitude shared by all the key members of our group. Whenever some serious problem came up which looked as if it might stop our progress, there was an immediate response of rallying around each other to analyze what we faced and begin an active search for a solution. And although there were many serious and unexpected obstacles to overcome, I do not recall the members of our group ever shaking their heads or being despondent. I don't know how much my own attitude (and perhaps naivete) influenced the group's approach. But I am now convinced that the way any innovator or entrepreneur faces adversity will affect the number, quality, and speed of possible solutions unleashed by the team.

This positive and aggressive approach to adversity has become so natural to me now that I have a great deal of difficulty when I see someone respond differently. I have a friend who had the habit of calling everyone he knew when adversity struck him or his business. He would describe the problem in gory detail—not to get help, but to "announce" that he was in a bad mess. Recently, this friend told me that he'd realized he did this to set up the dramatic situation so that he'd have an appreciative audience when he made an amazing recovery (which he often did). He said it had worked for a while, but he hadn't calculated the negative effect of his horror stories on his own staff, some of whom got tired of the game and left.

But when I'm tempted to get smug about the way we handled adversity, I keep reminding myself that I have had to *learn* what to do when adversity strikes. When I filled the Houston intersection with Coca Cola and broken glass, I began to learn to calmly "clean up the mess." When I realized my seven-hundred-home garbage truck only held the garbage from two hundred homes, I learned to aggressively seek solutions. And I'm still looking for new positive ways of handling adversity.

Reassessing the Possibilities

In the first few chapters of this section, I described how to make a preliminary investigation of an entrepreneurial venture. And I am convinced that by really examining the circumstances in a business and paying very careful attention to financing, experience needs, etc., much of what is called "adversity" can be avoided altogether.

But obviously, some will come, and when it does, having done that original investigation and planning can give you a structure in which new directions can more easily be found.

That's actually what happened to my young friend who put everything he had in the motel and had the highway moved away from him. After looking at what had happened, he realized that his action plan for a motel operation had been effectively destroyed by the moving of the highway and the new motel project at the cut-off point. But in his investigation of the city before buying the motel, he had noticed that there were many older people and almost no nursing home facilities. That information had been useful in determining possible sources of customers for his motel. But now, in going back through his evaluations of the city, he decided to make an action plan for converting the motel into a geriatric center. And as he investigated this possibility, he found that he could get some government funding, and he was back on track in what may have been an even more satisfying and lucrative venture than his first plan.

Realistically speaking, there will of course be times when, in spite of all your positive thinking and best efforts, you will fail to achieve your goals. When this happens, some people just throw up their hands in despair. But of course this is self-defeating. The best thing I know to do—as hard as it is sometimes—is to evaluate the situation and make an action plan to salvage all you can from the present venture. Then move on to another opportunity.

This kind of failure happened to me when I got divorced and left Browning-Ferris to work on several other ventures. Browning-Ferris stock was selling at approximately thirty dollars per share at the time of my divorce. I borrowed a substantial amount of money, using the stock as collateral, in making the divorce settlement. Actually, I only borrowed on a very small percent of the stock's value. But about a year later the value of the stock dropped to four dollars a share, due to several internal and external factors which hit at once. And overnight I was really in hot water financially, since the value of my stock was suddenly much less than I would need to repay the large amount of money I'd borrowed.

After receiving the shock, I assessed the situation, set new goals, and made an action plan. I put together an investment group and arranged to get my debts taken care of. I was afraid, and yet I knew I had to go forward with my plans without the security of the BFI stock. I made a new commitment, and then worked very hard to meet my goals and move forward. The experience of being able to "come back" after this period of serious adversity was what made me realize the power of the creative enterprise process.

As I reread these words, I realize that it *sounds* a lot easier to regroup and go forward than it actually *is* for me sometimes—in the face of uncertainty and the gnawing fear that I may be about to fail. But as difficult as it is, it is never as hard as I *fear* it is going to be to maintain the attitude that "we are going to overcome whatever obstacles come up."

But what we are talking about in describing the handling of adversity like this is part of a certain approach to management. What would the management style of a leader who faced problems this way be?

Chapter 19

AN APPROACH TO ORGANIZATIONAL MANAGEMENT

If your particular vocational venture is not a business with employees, you may have difficulty understanding how this chapter and the following two chapters relate to your personal situation. However, I urge you to stay with me, because there are some principles here which have changed my whole approach to people. And it's possible that some of them may apply to you as you seek to develop creative personal relationships in every area of your life. I am convinced that anyone whose personal and vocational success depends on working with other people can be helped considerably by coming to understand a little about the art of managing people in the arena of creative enterprise.

Actually, there are two stages in the life of a business or other corporate enterprise, and these stages require different approaches to management. "Organizational management" is involved in the first stage, the putting together and building of a venture. "Operational management" takes over in the second stage, the maintenance of the organization after it is securely established. In this chapter I will concentrate on management during the building stage, and I will describe a particular approach to management which I found to be very helpful in a rapidly developing situation.

The Managerial Squad—A Team Approach

Everyone likes the opportunity to hit the homerun in business. As I suggested in the chapter on capital, many people choose to do this through the use of heavy financial leverage. However, I believe it is possible and desirable to hit the really long ball by organizing for aggressive growth.

But organizing for growth on a large scale requires a division of the major responsibilities with a great deal of freedom of action for the manager of each area. At BFI, we found the best way to provide for this was to adopt a team approach to management, one which allowed for maximum autonomy on the part of each manager and which called for an unusual amount of cooperation and basic honesty toward each other, along with a minimum of selfishness and jockeying for position.

To use the team approach we found that the leader must be able to enjoy being surrounded by very capable and aggressive people without being overly threatened. He or she must be willing to share the *authority* in a real way, as well as the responsibility. And the open give-and-take of a genuine team situation must be something in which the leader can participate wholeheartedly without continually interjecting his "authority." *

We developed this team management approach during our growth-by-acquisition period by dividing the entire responsibility for the company into three distinct areas—development, administration, and management—and by making a different person totally responsible for each area. Lou Waters, Harry Phillips, and I each ran our own area almost as if it were a separate company, although we cooperated closely. We did institute a process of reviewing major decisions by all team members (usually after they were made), but at that point there was virtually no "second guessing" of each other or "attacking" people who made mistakes. The review was for the purpose of information and avoiding future mistakes.

All three of the basic areas were broken down into several more areas of responsibility, each of which would be made the responsibility of one person. This meant that before long our basic organizational management team was made up of thirteen members and looked something like the following:

---

* In the next chapter I will discuss in more detail the role and approach of the leader in a team management situation.

Team Management Plan—BFI

Executive officers: Harry Phillips
Lou Waters
Tom Fatjo

Development	*Administration*	*Management*
Tom Fatjo	Lou Waters	Harry Phillips
Acquisitions	Finance	Operating personnel
Market development	Accounting	Engineering
Sales	Legal management	Insurance
Corporate affairs		

Each person reporting to Harry, Lou, and me had almost autonomously handled responsibilities.

Once the team was formed and began to operate, the team members provided much, if not most, of the corrective input required to adjust the action plans and meet the goals. As the action plans unfolded, the management team stayed in close touch, discussing problems and their solutions and keeping each other informed about how the different divisions were working.

This team system of management worked very well for us. We found that an experienced team can function in this kind of framework with a minimum of checks and controls. And we learned that talented people, when given more autonomy, react much more for the good of the team than we would have thought at first.

Another advantage to this approach was that often a management team member would be able to bring very creative insights and solutions to problems brought up in another person's area of responsibility. By having some emotional distance from the stress of the problem, another manager could see at once something which the one responsible for the problem area couldn't see at all.

But having a group of talented and independently proven people on the same team also meant that we faced some very complicated human dynamics. I've since found that some of these problems can crop up in any team management situation. The team approach requires a great deal of openness and the willingness to face difficulties and shortcomings quickly and directly. And human pride is such that it is sometimes very difficult for a person who has been a star in his or her own operation to be a part of a team and not receive the deference he or she is used to. It can also be very threatening to high-achieving managers to let other managers constructively analyze *their* progress and methods. So there were a few bruised egos as we made the adjustment to the team approach.

I will say, however, that after the initial fear most of our team members really liked the approach. They liked having autonomous responsibility in their individual areas, and they soon saw that, in the team meetings, no one was attacked personally as we discussed results and the best ways to achieve them. It soon became clear, when we used this approach, that errors were corrected much more quickly and progress made more dependably. In a year's time, nearly everyone was won over.

For the several years which followed, the cooperative attitudes and mutual respect of the "building team" members as they entered the first stages of management was very exciting. There were unexpected benefits as we saw individuals accomplish goals in the team context they probably wouldn't have been able to reach on their own.

For example, Norman Myers was in charge of our acquisition program. And although Norman has great talent, I cannot imagine his being able to provide the leadership for an acquisition program the size of BFI alone—he just did not have the experience. As a matter of fact, no one did. But he listened, learned from everyone on the team, and as a result he probably participated in more corporate acquisitions than anyone in the world from 1970 to 1972.

Team Effort Can Accomplish Significant Goals

As I said in an earlier chapter, my choice of a team approach to management may have come from an extremely vivid awareness of my own shortcomings and the consequent need to draw on others' abilities and experiences. But I had been fascinated to see how effective team efforts have been in recent world history.

I think this notion of using a team to accomplish large goals came home to modern historians in a striking way after the bombing of Pearl Harbor. The way Americans cooperated to build a war machine astonished the world—particularly Germany and Japan. People couldn't imagine our producing one hundred thousand planes and numberless tanks, guns, and bombs. We really did become the "arsenal of democracy."

I personally began to see the implications of a team or squad approach to entrepreneurial efforts when John Kennedy made the commitment to send a man to the moon. It was not easy. After the goals were set and the plans made there were some frustrating months. The early problems in trying to catch up with the Russian space effort were considerable—and complex. With early failures came despondency. But in spite of these things the project grew. The unfolding of separate action plans and their amazing final coordination—culminated when, as the world watched in awe, Neil Armstrong stepped out of the space ship onto the surface of the moon. In spite of the confusion and frustration, all of the teamwork which went into reaching that goal made me realize that with clear goals, good planning, and a solid management approach, most anything could be accomplished.

As I thought of both these examples (the war effort and the moon shot), I remember wondering, "What was it which allowed these thousands of talented men and women to work together in such a creative way?" Of course, in both cases, some were paid very well for participating. But that payment doesn't begin to account for the intensity of the effort and the kind of cooperation achieved. No, the crucial factor seems to have been that the team members were emotionally caught up in a cause which was bigger than their personal plans.

A friend of Bud Wilkinson, the former head coach of the University of Oklahoma football team, told me that Wilkinson's success was achieved in large measure because he was a master at getting his individual players to give their best for the benefit of the entire team. Every year at the first practice, he used to ask the new players, "How many of you can name the All-American team members of four years ago?" No one could name more than a few. Then he asked them, "How many of you can name the number-one *team* in the nation four years ago?" And almost all of them had the answer—not just for one year, but for several. Wilkinson went on to say, in effect, "If you want to be remembered for excellence, be a part of a championship team!"

Sacrifice, a Natural Ingredient of Teamwork

Really creative teamwork comes when the members of a management group see themselves as being a part of an adventure they conceive of as being more important, more glamorous, and more meaningful than whatever they were doing before. In the early stages of a creative enterprise, I believe it is almost more important to choose people with this "commitment to the cause" attitude than individuals with superior capabilities who don't feel that way.

As a part of their participation, the team members must want the dream enough to be willing to sacrifice the immediate ego satisfaction of being treated as prima donnas. There is no room for prima donnas in the formative team effort—no matter how outstanding a job an individual may be doing.

As a matter of fact, in business, having a championship team can call for some stark sacrificing of personal prestige in order to make things happen the way they should.

At Browning-Ferris there have been many such sacrifices of position. One of the most apparent was that made by Granville Deane. Granville's father had been one of the top executives of Browning-Ferris Machinery Company for many years before we acquired it in 1969. Granville and his family owned approximately 30 percent of the stock, and his entire business career had been with the company.

For many years Granville had been the sales manager in the Houston office, and when we purchased controlling interest, he became president of Browning-Ferris Industries. But when we started the aggressive acquisition of solid-waste companies, the complexion, the balance, and the purpose of our efforts all began to change drastically almost overnight. It wasn't long before BFI was primarily a solid-waste company rather than a distributor of heavy equipment, as it had been before the acquisition.

Because of this change, it became apparent that we should sell the machinery company, and that Harry Phillips should become president of Browning-Ferris Industries to help integrate and manage the burgeoning solid-waste company we were becoming. Granville saw the situation and did not hesitate to step aside. Of course, he did have a large investment in the company, and his move represented a good investment decision for him. But as any experienced leader can tell you, when a manager's ego is involved it is often very difficult for him or her to set aside the personal need for prestige and ego-fulfillment for the benefit of the project—even if doing so might further his or her investment.

I know that expecting this kind of sacrifice may sound utopian. But whether you are engaged in starting a small venture with a few people or are manager of a new subsidiary of a major corporation, there seems to be a period during the organization and building phase of management in which the threat of failure is still strong enough to allow an honesty-and-cooperation-for-survival approach to work. I have been amazed at the sacrifical effort people will make when it seems they can share significantly in causing the goals to be reached. (This situation may change when the shift to operational management is made. We will discuss the nature of this change in chapters 22 and 24.)

Choosing Team Members

I suppose my own personality needs originally dictated my choice of team members, but I have come to believe that there is a certain type of person who can work far better within a team context than others. This kind of person must like to run his or her own shop and be willing to make important decisions. But he or she must also like to work within a larger structure for which he or she is not totally responsible.

For example, I know a man who is a very talented and creative executive. He's vice president of a substantial corporation. There is no question in my mind that this man could run his own company; he is not afraid of decisions and is very aggressive. As a matter of fact, he has been approached by several groups of investors to start new companies. But when it got right down to the point of leaving, this man told a mutual friend, "I just don't want to be responsible for the whole show."

On the other hand, there is a certain kind of person who cannot tolerate structure unless it is self-designed and self-imposed. People like this are loners, and they don't want to do anything unless *they* thought of it. This latter sort of man or woman will not do for a team management approach. But neither will the bright and talented person who cannot make crucial independent decisions regarding his or her part of the larger venture. So the ideal person is the one who has the natural ability and brains to run his or her own show, but who prefers to work in context with larger purposes and goals.

Sometimes, in the process of recruiting, it is hard to tell if someone will be a good team member or not. But as the project moves forward, it usually doesn't take long to find out. The new employee may start out as a team member, but soon begin trying to take over (or climb over) other people for his or her own benefit. When this happens, action must be taken at once to stop such moves, because the team approach to management absolutely depends on the cooperative attitude of the different members.

Team Management Works—But Not Always!

Since the team approach worked so remarkably well in the launching stage of Browning-Ferris Industries, I tried it several times—in other ventures. And now I am even more convinced that the right group, properly motivated and working together, can accomplish almost anything.

Having said this, let me state clearly that there are times when a team approach is *not* good. This is especially true in an emergency. In making this point recently, a friend of mine said that if a group of crack pilots were flying in a Boeing 727 and all engines went out at once, then whether they used the team approach to solve the problem would depend on how high they were flying. Since the Boeing 727 evidently has a glide ratio of about seventeen to one, if the plane were flying at forty thousand feet it would glide about one hundred fifty miles. In that case the team approach might be used. But if the plane were flying at two thousand feet, my friend said he would hope someone understood the single-executive model of management.

I realize that certain elements of the approach we used at BFI worked because of the specific circumstances and might not be effective in many situations. Actually, the whole approach was designed for accomplishing a substantial number of goals in a short period of time. But I do believe that certain aspects of the team model of organizational management can offer almost unlimited potential for creativity and flexibility. But in order for it to work, the innovator-leader must really believe in the approach, and must understand clearly what his or her role in the process is. In the next chapter, we will look at the leader's place in the team approach to organizational management.

Chapter 20

THE LEADER'S ROLE—VULNERABLE TOUGHNESS

I am fully aware that my own management style grew out of a very unusual situation in which I knew less than several of the management team members about the business we were in at BFI. But I have since used the same approach to management in the formation of several other businesses, and I find that the results seem to be very positive.

Since we had such an experienced and capable group of people on the Browning-Ferris team, I tried to conduct the meetings as one of the group on the adventure—not as "the boss" or the "one who knew." In the first place, I *didn't* know as much as the individual members did about their areas. And in the second place, a part of my own necessary training to be able to guide and coordinate the various action plans depended on my learning everything I could about each area of the business as it developed. So I asked questions and listened when I didn't know something, and this seemed to help create a climate in which each manager felt safe in expressing his own questions and problems without the fear of being shot down or sabotaged by his fellow managers.

I have come to believe that such an attitude on the part of the innovator or leader is the key to making team management work. Whether you are starting a small venture or are president of a major corporation, you, the leader, are the *only* one who can effectively make the team approach work. It's frightening for managers to risk being open about their work. And, in order to create an atmosphere in which proud, aggressive men and women can express questions, take suggestions and be open for criticism, you must be willing to ask for, and receive, the same thing from others. Without your honest modeling of the team approach, I am convinced that no one else will risk being vulnerable. It may seem like a tough price to pay, but without it there is little hope for any creatively vulnerable cooperation.

This way of operating can be very tricky. In large organizations many people have come a long way in the corporate jungle by learning to be merciless predators whose competitive instincts have been honed to a fine edge. Such persons often view any vulnerability or openness on the part of another manager as a weakness. And they may jump on an honest, vulnerable admission as an opportunity to climb by capitalizing on a "weakness" or unguarded statement in a team meeting.

Most people in corporate situations know the danger from "jungle fighters," and have learned to protect themselves. (They may have done some jungle fighting themselves!) But this kind of attitude can destroy a team approach. So it's up to the leader to set the tone for openness and give-and-take. The key to team members' being willing to risk vulnerability is, I repeat, for you the leader to ask for and be willing to receive the same kind of help you are hoping the others will exchange.

It *is* true that you as the founder or leader of a company must remain in some kind of ultimate position of control, if you are responsible for the setting and meeting of the goals the venture is based on. But when it comes to the actual working plans, you must be as open and vulnerable as everyone else on the team. When you have been challenged on an idea and have seen that the alternate suggestion is better than your own plan—*and actually changed the plan* in accordance with the new idea, you will become more credible to the other team members. Then they may be willing to risk being open.

Delegating Authority

One of the common misconceptions about entrepreneurs is the idea that they are daring, strong, extroverted, and sometimes careless. On the other hand, professional managers are thought to be dotters of *i*'s and crossers of *t*'s. But the research on executive behavior by David C. McClelland *et al* at Harvard * has suggested that the *entrepreneur* is more likely to be the dotter of *i*'s and the crosser of *t*'s. He or she most likely has some of the same motivational patterns as the artist. The entrepreneurial type, like the artist, is motivated by the need for achievement and is strongly compelled to put all the finishing touches on the product or service. And like the artist, he or she has the need for *closure*—seeing the whole thing finished and perfect, with all the *t*'s and *i*'s crossed and dotted right down to the final one.

But the danger in this sort of perfectionism is that many entrepreneurs or innovators cannot really delegate. They can only assign, and they keep a tight watch on the work so as to insure it's being done their way. So when it comes to management—either organizational or operational—the entrepreneur or innovator can become the growing company's own greatest enemy. This is true because one person can personally oversee only a limited number of projects and details. So to build or manage a venture of any size, you must learn to turn loose of as many details and decisions as possible.

I know from personal experience how difficult it can be for an entrepreneur to allow people the freedom to make important decisions on their own. But I've got to say again that this is *essential* if any large venture is to succeed. The freedom of the managers to "suggest and change" is perceived as real by the team members *only* if they *really are* allowed a great deal of freedom in the day-to-day operation of their particular segments of the company.

If you as the entrepreneur-leader become too involved in each particular area of the business, feeling you have to dot all the *i*'s personally, you may get caught with your head buried in one stack of papers when a destructive fire breaks out in another manager's action plan.

In the developmental stage of BFI, I actually took one management section as my own responsibility and became, in that

* David C. McClelland, *The Achieving Society* (New York: Free Press, 1967).

instance, sort of a player-coach. Sometimes this may be necessary. But if you do get involved in one particular area, you also have to maintain an overall view or perspective from which you can be a knowing participant in each phase of the company's development.

This second overall perspective, a more removed vantage point from which to see the whole operation, is essential. It has to be as if your attention mechanism has a zoom lens you can adjust in an instant so as to allow undivided concentration on a specific problem as if there were nothing else on your mind. But then when that problem has been handled, you must be able to zoom back to the larger perspective and see how what has just happened fits into the overall picture.

This may seem to be a very demanding way to run a business, and of course it is. But it is much less demanding in my judgment than the single-executive-officer plan, in which the entrepreneur functions alone or with one or two trusted advisors. With their input, he attempts to make decisions and plans which I believe can better be made by other executives in the company who have far more know-how in their specialized areas. I've found that once a top management person gets accustomed to the team approach there is much less pressure to be "the one who knows everything." And the increased productivity which can result from a team management style of this kind makes all the managers look good—including the person at the top.

Ego Problems and Prima Donnas

No one likes to talk about the way ego problems can erode the creative life of a large corporation, a government agency, or a religious institution, because who of us is free from this pernicious self-centeredness? But many companies find their original enthusiasm and sense of mission evaporating because of a few men or women who seem to feel the need to become little kings or queens in executive suites.

There are several kinds of "prima donna" behavior that can sabotage a team operation. One manager may misunderstand the "being one of the team" behavior of the leader, and may try to step into what he or she views as a power vacuum to take control of the organization. Another kind of prima donna will expect to be treated with special deference and not want to abide by the agreed-upon ways of conducting the team approach.

Both kinds of behavior must be stopped firmly at a very early stage by the leader of the organization. A power-grabbing manager cannot be tolerated. If a private explanation of the team approach goes unheeded, he or she must be taken off the team. (Of course, "taking someone off the team" is difficult to do, particularly if there was a hard negotiation to get the manager on the team in the first place. But if you deal quickly and firmly with prima-donna behavior the first time it shows up in your team, you'll probably never have to do it again.)

If "star performers" who want special treatment can't adjust to the give-and-take atmosphere of team management, the solution is the same—face it with them and say "good-by." There is too much at stake to have the main agenda be the assuaging of ruffled feelings—even though a leader should always try to be sensitive to the honest difficulties a proven star has in being a member of a new team.

Of course, entrepreneur-leaders aren't immune to the problems of ego, either. And when a leader begins to protect his or her position, it becomes very difficult for that leader to dream new dreams or recognize new opportunities. It's harder for him or her to become caught up in the desire to accomplish significant new goals. I was once able to acquire a company just because the president of that company was more interested in perks for himself than in progress. All the other owners got together and sold the controlling interest, because they were afraid of being stuck with a president who was just looking out for his personal needs and desires.

So once more I repeat that I believe the key to having the cooperative magic happen is for the leader himself or herself to be a member of the team without special "social" privileges in the carrying on of business.*

* I know how hard this is to do, and I realize that some entrepreneurs could not operate this way comfortably. But for me this approach, which in some ways is the opposite of the traditional one, has worked very well.

One of the most useful by-products of the "managerial squad" team approach is that it cuts down the likelihood of the "halo effect" that can occur once an innovator has succeeded in a given field. Colleagues may be too quick to rubber stamp or accept a leader's proposed plans uncritically, they may assume (or allow the entreprenuer to assume) that he or she can walk on water. Unfortunately, at times a little success can cause most of us to get an inflated notion of our capability. But with a squad of independent, aggressive managers this is *very* unlikely. After a basic honesty has been established in a team situation, such claims will simply not be supported—as they often are in some management situations.

As I read back through these last two chapters, I am well aware that I will appear to be very naive to many leaders who have become cynical about people's willingness to sacrifice their desires for the top star billing in order to have a part in building something significant. And of course it is true that many people simply don't care about anything except their immediate gratification.

But I have found that there is a breed of men and women in America who *want* to throw their vocational lives into large dreams and reach out for seemingly impossible goals. The secret is of course that you as the top person *must want these things too.* And if you do, then you may find great untapped power in the most surprising people through the team approach to organizational management.

It is very important to recognize that the management principles and procedures we have been describing in the last two chapters only apply to the very aggressive growth period—the first stage of an enterprise. Once a certain plateau is reached, many aspects of stage-one management become inappropriate. Actually, it's a little bit like organizing for war. When the war is over, many of the soldiers have to go home, and the occupational forces arrive to help "consolidate the victory." Then begins the changeover to operational management, which will be the subject of the next chapter.

Chapter 21

TRANSITION TO OPERATIONAL MANAGEMENT

As far as I am concerned, the ultimate test of success for a fully launched creative venture is the subsequent development of a *continuing* profitable or effective and well-disciplined enterprise. So many rapidly built companies fall apart after a short time. And all the pain and heartache of the developing process will be for nothing if the company does not develop into a profitable, well-operated and continuing business. The same principle applies to a professional career or a social or religious institution.

In almost any business (or other institution) the transition into "major company" operating management can be extremely unsettling and threatening for an entrepreneur-innovator. There is an excitement about the life and death struggles of "fighting a war" which is missing for some people in the subsequent process of "winning the peace." Many people in leadership positions have trouble changing perspectives in order to consolidate the gains made through the organizational phase. In fact, there may be certain aspects of this new phase which are not readily compatible with the temperaments and motives of many entrepreneur-innovators.

Builders and Managers

This constitutes a problem that must be confronted by founders of creative enterprises, whether they are businesses, churches, hospitals, or other institutions. The people who are the best *managers* of ongoing enterprises often have certain distinctly different characteristics and drives from those of the entrepreneur-founders.

Psychologist David McClelland and his associates * have found three dominant motives among adults: the need for affiliation or love, the need for power, and the need for achievement. While it is difficult to generalize, the entrepreneur is usually motivated by the need for achievement. As I suggested earlier, this can mean he or she will tend to keep close control of an operation because of an obsession with the product. This obsession to "get it right regardless of cost" can become entangled in one's ego, and if this happens the entrepreneur can make serious financial and managerial mistakes.

The professional manager, on the other hand, seems to need power for its own sake. He or she needs not so much to control the product as to control the people. Someone with this kind of motivation may be better able to maintain stability and productivity in an ongoing business or institution.

In saying this, I may seem to be picturing the professional manager as a power-hungry ogre. But while that may be true in some instances, it is certainly not a universal condition of managers. From a manager's perspective, power is the tool necessary to bring discipline and order out of the aftermath of the creative thrust which culminated in the formation or consolidation of the business.

I have a business associate, Tom Tierney, who has said many times that "there are builders and there are managers, but there are seldom builder-managers." I know from looking at my own feelings that there is a tendency for some of us to think we can be both. But for the long haul I believe Tom is right. And the entrepreneur-builder who might think he or she is different and able to perform both functions efficiently might do well to seek some outside advice—or at least to recognize and compensate for his or her relative weakness in the operational

---

* David C. McClelland and David H. Burnham, "Power-Driven Managers: Good Guys Make Bum Bosses," *Psychology Today* 9, no. 7 (December 1975).

phase. And in a large venture it seems to me that the entrepreneur would do well to have some professional manager types to help make the transition from the organizational phase of management to the operational.

Making the Transition

At BFI, we found the transition from a posture of aggressive growth to major company management could be a reasonably orderly one, although it wasn't always easy or devoid of problems. To make the changeover, we kept our basic organization, but changed the functions of each division. Our *development* segment (acquisitions, market development, sales, and corporate affairs) became fully occupied with sales and marketing. All of our *administrative* departments (finance, accounting, legal management) became staff functions. And in the *management* area we developed additional depth in each subsection and changed our concentration from integrating new companies to developing uniformly efficient operations in all areas.

In 1973, when these emphasis changes had been made, we started a market development program. As a part of the goal setting and action planning for this new phase of our corporate management life, we initiated a system of regional vice presidents. Our action plan was designed to gather from each of our one hundred thirty companies the best operational methods, customer relations procedures, sales and marketing plans, and internal development approaches within each city.

Harry Phillips, the president of BFI, along with a strong office staff, collected and refined the information as it was gathered. And they, along with the team of regional vice presidents, constructed a consistent operating approach to all areas of our business. The new approach included the best of any one company in any area, plus some new ideas which came as a result of combining all the most efficient methods.

After working the bugs out of the resulting procedures, we developed a controllable consistency of policies. The regional vice presidents adapted the new plans in their own areas within the commonly-agreed-upon procedures. And we saw a regularity and orderliness develop within the whole company in a very short time.

New Management Requirements

With these changes in the general structure of BFI came a different set of management requirements. Instead of the needs for imagination and creativity being primary, we were now looking for solid, practical, and consistent decision-making.

This need for a different kind of management occurs in most companies that are in the process of transition from rapid growth to ongoing operation. And it can bring on some problems. When the restless, creative trail-boss-buffalo-hunter type of leader is asked to stop and supervise the farming of the land like a settler, he or she may not be able to make the adjustment without running off a good many new settlers—it is very discouraging to have someone drive a herd of wild buffalo through the field you are trying to cultivate! Fortunately, we had some "buffalo hunters" who were ready to settle after the acquisition period, and others went on to fresh territory outside the company.

At the top executive level, we made some changes, too. Up to this point Harry Phillips, Lou Waters, and I had been co-executive officers. But after three years of the transition period into the operational phase, I resigned as an officer. I was starting a new business but stayed active as a member of the board of BFI.

After another two years Harry Phillips became the sole chief executive officer, and Lou Waters continued as chairman of the board. With these management changes, most of the transition from the acquisition building team to the operational management team were virtually completed. And, as I mentioned earlier, from 1973 to 1980 the management team and new plans took the annual sales to $552 million.

A Team Approach to *Operational* Management

Of course, there are many effective ways to structure major company management and to make the necessary transition from acquisition and growth to long-range operations. We kept to our team approach, although team management requires much time and effort in clarifying short-term goals and how they relate to major long-term goals. Good communication is essential with a team approach, and we found this is both difficult and time consuming.

It is true, however, that the more usual entrepreneurial pattern of a strong founder at the top with a group of professional managers just below him is also difficult to work out successfully. Frequently in such an organization there is a conflict between the entrepreneur, who sees through an aggressive-expansive organizational lens, and the managers, who have consolidating, order-producing lenses.

Actually, there is no reason either approach cannot work if there is adequate communication and if the management team is allowed to make its own decisions without being constantly corrected and second-guessed by a restless entrepreneur. Many times, in order to keep from being bored, an entrepreneur-innovator will start a new venture in the midst of the established one, just as the need for consolidation is at its highest in the existing company. And if this happens, many managers will despair at ever getting the necessary controls established to have a smoothly running organization.

Dealing with Jealousy and Resentment

The process of maturation and consolidation I have described can be a very logical process. But, as I have already pointed out in a dozen ways in this book, logic is not always the ruling force in the creative enterprise process. When the excitement of the "acquisition and growth" wars is over, some very human and very powerful factors can begin to surface—factors which if not handled properly can destroy a lot of what the building team has put together through the heat of the battle.

Perhaps the most difficult of these factors to deal with is emerging jealousy among the team members. It is unfortunate that, during this transition, many people are not at all content simply to take pride in their accomplishments and capabilities. Often something occurs which is reminiscent of the generals from ancient Rome who fought well together during a war but then bickered over the division of the spoils after the victory was won. When the excitement of the initial adventure dies down, the individual dreams and ambitions of each team member will likely surface and may begin to take precedence over the "common cause."

I believe this is one of those situations that can best be handled by "an ounce of prevention." An entrepreneur will do much better at this stage if he or she has not made veiled promises of glory and position when wooing people to join the building team. A straightforward pitch about the adventure and a statement that "we'll have to work out the future as it unfolds" leaves less room for misunderstanding and jealousy later (unless of course the entrepreneur *intends* to make a specific commitment to an individual team member). As the growth and development progress, the entrepreneur will do well to be very clear with people concerning appointments and promotions and stay away from vagueness in the area of "promises."

But regardless of how careful one is to be honest when negotiating with people on the team, there will always be some who will assume promises which fit their unspoken fantasies. That is just a part of the difficulty of communication between human beings which complicates the creative enterprise process at every turn. And the only "cure" I know of is to stay in close touch with each team member—especially in the transition period. The problems of jealousy and disappointment will have to be worked out, on a one-to-one basis, to the best of the leader's ability.

A Change Must Take Place

It hasn't been my intention in this chapter to offer a detailed description of the operational management process. Rather, my primary purpose is to make it absolutely clear that some sort of change *must* take place. Although I realize that different companies will develop in very different ways, I believe that a maturing and consolidating process something like the one I have described must take place sooner or later or the twin dangers of overhead and operational inefficiency will devour the bottom line.

Large companies cannot be run like small growing ones. Mature companies cannot be managed like those that are going through an aggressive period of development. For instance, during the acquisition period at BFI it would have been madness to try to standardize all operational procedures in over one hundred companies—as we were acquiring them. We had a central reporting system to allow for the overall financial and management decisions to be intelligently reviewed, and just enough centralized procedures to allow us to keep our balance, but there was no way at that time to institute detailed procedures for uniform management.

We were trying, it seemed, to stay on top of an enormous snowball that was careening down a mountain, doubling its size every few turns. It was only after the snowball stopped that we were able to turn to a refining and standardizing of all procedures. But then we had to make that transition *at once* in order to capitalize on the combined experience we had acquired—to keep the snowball from melting.

It is in fact this change to an orderly management process which really provides the opportunity for the entrepreneur's original dream to come true. But, paradoxically, it is often his or her own lack of awareness of the need for a change in management goals which causes the entrepreneur to resist and even kill the transition which could save and complete the dream.

Chapter 22

DEALING WITH ERRORS IN JUDGMENT

A shining new bank building, theater, or cathedral, filled with sharp-looking men and women, *looks* almost perfect. But anyone on the inside of such a project knows that, unseen by the public, dozens if not hundreds of errors in judgment were made along the way, as the project was being built and developed. I'm convinced that this is true of the work of *every* entrepreneur or manager who builds or operates a large institution.

There is a commonly held fantasy abroad that people who do anything *really well* make almost no errors. But that is simply untrue. I remember clearly the jolt I felt as a young man when I realized that the greatest professional baseball players in history were put out before they reached first base *more than 60 percent of the time.* How many great quarterbacks have completed more than six out of ten of their passes during their careers? Or how many basketball players hit more than half of their shots? And contrary to much public opinion, many of the most outstanding businesses in the world operate with a clear understanding that only *a very small percent* of their efforts will be successful.

For example, even with the best geologists, major oil companies only find producible oil in *one* wildcat well out of *nine* or *ten* drilled; the rest are "failures." In the direct mail business, with all its market research, a response of 4 percent to a mail-out is considered great. That means 96 percent of the people contacted fail to respond. And highly trained insurance salesman chalk up many failures for every successful sale.

These kinds of "failures" are most generally attributed to unknown factors or unforeseen circumstances involved in finding oil, selling by direct mail, and locating really live insurance prospects, for instance. But many of the failures come from simple errors in judgment. And often in a creative enterprise, whether or not the overall dream of the originator is successfully realized depends on how these errors are faced and dealt with.

What Is an Error in Judgment?

My working definition of an "error in judgment" is simply a circumstance which turns out wrong and hinders progress as a result of a management decision. No one likes to make a mistake. And it is even less satisfying to admit having made a costly one. But if such errors are faced openly from the beginning, they can become a constructive energizing force for future effectiveness.

Most people know this. But I find a strong tendency in myself to look for a reason *outside* me and my decisions for any circumstances which turn out wrong. I always hope there is something or someone besides me at fault. And I'm often tempted to put the blame on someone else, even when I know I've blown it.

I am continually amazed at the lengths to which I and other people will go to protect our egos when we make a wrong decision. Sometimes we imply that no other "intelligent" decision could have been made. Many times I have said, or heard other people say, for instance, "If I had the same opportunity to make the same decision with the same facts, I would make the same decision!" But the basic truth is that, when things go wrong, often a wrong decision has been made which might well have been avoided.

Many people will object to my saying this and point out (as I did earlier) that *every* executive will make errors in judgment because no one can be aware of all the facts, and because there are always circumstances that are beyond the decider's control. Of course there *will* be some circumstances beyond anyone's control. But that's not the issue. The point I am making here is that a *self-justifying attitude* in dealing with errors in judgment is crippling and self-defeating. And it can not only stop the process of getting back on track but can poison the progress of an organization so that the ultimate goal cannot be reached.

People in leadership positions often go to almost suicidal lengths to avoid saying the words, "I was wrong." I am convinced that, even at the height of the Watergate scandal, the American public would have forgiven Richard Nixon if he could have said clearly and without equivocation: "I was wrong in my judgment and actions and I am responsible." But as far as I know he never did.

Much enervating rehashing is done every day in creative enterprises by people trying to save their pride when they have made a wrong decision. (Of course, there *is* a time for honestly trying to learn how a faulty decision was made so as not to repeat it, but this exercise should *not* be for the purpose of self-justification.)

Why do we insist so on being right—even if it destroys our dreams or sometimes our integrity? I think one reason is deeply embedded in today's culture. We have a horror of looking stupid. And as a people we are trained from childhood (either by parents or TV) to hide our imperfections "cosmetically" or through appearing to be successful. But what often comes across to us as children is the message, "Don't make mistakes. People will not forgive you, and you'll fail!" So we learn at an early age to hide or deny our errors in judgment. And by the time we are adults we can't admit our failures, because we feel that we'll be judged and condemned *as persons* if we are caught in a costly error.

In business I believe that some entrepreneurs and managers aggravate this problem. They try to frighten people into making fewer mistakes by "not forgiving them" (or by firing them) when they make wrong decisions. But this attitude is not only counterproductive; it is also at the most basic level *irrational.* To put a moral coloring on errors in judgment—so that people somehow feel condemned for making an error of any kind—is like condemning a batter for being put out or a football player for being tackled. I am convinced that such an attitude—which is all too common in some organizations—causes *more* instead of *fewer* errors and leads to the *hiding* of many important mistakes.

An Alternative Approach

As a young boy I learned that we Christians believe, if we confess our sins and mistakes to God and to the people we've offended, that God not only will forgive us but will also give us a completely new start. And I believed that this was the way God wanted things done. The problem, though, was that I wasn't sure *the people I offended* believed in forgiveness as much as I did. So I hated to admit my wrong actions to *people*. And I found that other people felt the same way about admitting mistakes.

But somewhere in my struggles to understand life, I began to see that the only hope to cure serious errors is to somehow get them out in the open. Hiding mistakes is like hiding cancer symptoms; it can lead to the death of the *whole organism*. I became convinced that this is especially true in business.

But how could I, as a leader, get the people in my organization to admit their errors so that the problems could be solved quickly and efficiently? How could the people around me trust my claim that I didn't condemn people who made errors in judgment? The only way I could find to make this claim believable was to admit my own errors when I discovered I'd made them. At the time, I didn't think all this through the way I'm describing it here. But I did start a policy of admitting my own mistakes to those around me. And when I did, I discovered a whole new kind of corporate power.

The Power from "Owning" Your Errors

If the top person can admit to making errors, a tremendous creative force may be released which will likely ripple to the very outer edges of a company. When a leader frankly admits making specific errors, the other team members may feel safe to admit their own mistakes. And once an error is recognized and admitted, it is possible to handle it and move forward immediately. But hiding errors, procrastinating, or trying to blame someone else or "circumstances beyond my control" only raises an emotional fog bank which stalls forward motion.

As I have suggested, the members of the organizational management team at BFI had a great deal of autonomy in carrying out their parts of the action plans. But after the acquisition of other companies began, we were in almost constant communications with each other. When something big went wrong, Lou, Harry, and I got together with the rest of the team immediately. And since we really trusted each other's abilities and commitment to meet our common goals, it didn't really matter to us who actually made the error. The point was to solve the problem which resulted from the mistake and then get on with building the company.

Because we had all worked together to formulate and check our plans, we felt a shared sense of responsibility and culpability when an error in judgment was revealed. In a real sense, we usually felt that we were *all* a part of any errors; they were team mistakes, not isolating individual ones. After several years of experience at BFI, we began to admit our errors more readily and therefore were able to make quicker and more efficient adjustments when things did not work out according to our plans. This approach was a new experience for most of us, but it worked. And the key to making it work was for whoever committed an error—even if it were the top person—to admit it.

At BFI we found this process helpful in dealing with even very significant errors in judgment. And we made some *big* mistakes. The largest that stands out in my mind was the decision to expand into the waste-paper or secondary-fiber industry. During late 1971 and early 1972, our company was handling approximately twelve million tons of waste annually. We found that this material was 70 percent paper by volume. Disposal costs were continuing to increase, so it seemed very logical to try to find a use for this paper that would reduce disposal costs and develop a new revenue stream. After some investigation, we decided to acquire the largest waste-paper company in the country.

After the acquisition of this company, our annual profits in waste paper went from approximately $400 thousand to almost $14 million in two years. But the year after that we lost approximately $6 million in waste paper alone. From $14 million *profit* to a $6 million *loss* in one division of a company whose total pretax earnings were approximately $30 million at the time was very significant.

What we hadn't counted on was what can happen to the waste-paper business during recessionary times. One year the sales may be enormous and the next year the bottom can fall out—regardless of skill and planning. We knew that much of the reprocessed waste paper goes into products relating to the building business, but what we didn't foresee was having the high prices we were committed to pay for waste paper tie into the worst building recession swing in anyone's memory. Not checking far enough to realize this could happen resulted in a very serious error in judgment. And we paid for the error in enormous loss of earnings.

Another serious error occurred when—almost in the beginning—we were appointed trustee in bankruptcy for a large company. Even though I didn't trust the owner after meeting him and talking to him, I decided that we should accept the appointment. I did this against my better judgment because I was eager to demonstrate what we could do as a company. The president turned out to be dishonest and sabotaged our efforts. We lost a lot of money, primarily because I ignored some very obvious warning signals and got tripped up by my own egotistical impatience to show the world "how great we were."

In the course of building BFI, I and other members of our management team made literally dozens of errors in judgment. And yet as we were making, learning from, and correcting these errors, we increased the company's annual sales from $250 thousand to more than $550 million. The number of strikeouts is not always the significant figure, although of course the percentages need to be watched. With talented players, it is the way the strikeouts are handled that really makes the difference.

A Creative Atmosphere

We learned that the willingness to be objective about one's own mistakes provides—as a by-product—a new atmosphere in business. This is a creative environment in which it is safe for anyone to *voice* new ideas—ideas which may sound outlandish at first but which could give the company a chance to make quantum leaps. I believe this happens because, when someone in a position of authority and responsibility is able to admit being wrong, everyone in the organization gets the idea that "being wrong" is not a capital offense or an occasion for making fun of the one who makes the mistake. This atmosphere creates a deep emotional security in which a manager may feel safe to try a variety of creative changes in his or her area of responsibility.

It may seem strange, to anyone who has never worked in a large organization, that talented employees—even managers—might be afraid to suggest creative new ways to do things as a means of achieving the organization's goals. But the fear of being wrong, of being considered foolish or impractical or of failing somehow may be the biggest deterrents to creativity in sizable corporations and other large organizations. And since creativity is one of the most valued qualities in the process we are describing, any way to foster a creative atmosphere is invaluable.

But, in creating an ambiance in which it is all right to confess errors—as with so many situations involving egotistical pride—the *behavior of the top visible leader* determines whether or not it will *really* be safe to be vulnerable in the ongoing life of an organization.

When a top manager is *not* willing to admit his or her own mistakes, an enormous coverup operation often results, in which hidden errors in judgment become malignant growths, often discovered too late to save the organization's life. And other members of the management team working with such a leader not only lose respect for him, but find a strange and fearful self-protectiveness coming into their work. Mistrust and stale inefficiency can replace the enthusiasm and creative energy with which the management team began the adventure.

But even with the best of leaders, the productive attitude of openness and vulnerability can be deeply and adversely affected by the growing success—and the consequent increase in power—which the leader may gain.

Chapter 23

AVOIDING THE ABUSE OF POWER

One of the most significant emotional difficulties which comes into play when one succeeds in the creative enterprise process concerns the handling of power.

The kind of process we've been discussing can generate a great deal of economic, political, and social power in a short time. And this is true whether the organization is a church or a large business. The leader who may have been just a "hard-working boy or girl" in his or her own mind can suddenly be shot into new financial and social orbits by economic or vocational success. This new power can be very creative and constructive in terms of one's relationships. Or, it can be almost demonic in its tendency to wreak emotional havoc in the lives of people around the entrepreneur. And this can happen without his or her ever realizing what took place!

Lord Acton said something to the effect that "power tends to corrupt and absolute power corrupts absolutely." I realize that some people may not think a discussion on the proper use of power is relevant with regard to creative ventures. But there are some facts about the nature of newly acquired power which, if not understood, can lead to broken relationships between people who have been working and/or living together for years.

The Subtle Change Success Can Bring

When the dust settles on a completed action plan and a goal has been reached, there is a possibility that one may undergo a very subtle and unconscious change in attitude toward self, family, and fellow workers. It is very easy to unconsciously begin to believe our own press clippings. With enough extravagant affirmation and material success, the most humble person in the world may begin to think, in moments alone, things like, "Well, maybe I *do* have special abilities—'genius' is probably too strong, but I must have *something* unusual or all this wouldn't be happening."

This may sound like egomania, but it happens to all kinds of basically unpretentious people. I have a friend who is a successful writer. After half a dozen best sellers in a row, this friend told me, he began to feel as if he had a "special gift." And he does have special talent. But as he discussed his problems and feelings, it became clear that he was concentrating on reader's responses to what he had written instead of on his writing. Because of this, he had began making unusual demands on his family and was hurt when they didn't seem thrilled about all the attention he was getting from his "fans." And his creative ability dried up, until he began to recognize that his egotistical preoccupation with his own achievements was destroying his ability to touch people through his work. Only then was he able to get a sense of balance about what was happening to him.

In saying this, I certainly don't want to imply that people should deny the reality of their abilities or achievements. But the subtle trap is that you, as the entrepreneur, may start taking your own abilities and opinions too seriously and taking special privileges for yourself. It's all too easy to make additional demands on the people closest to you in a way that may indicate to them that you think they *owe* it to you to give up their own agendas and goals for you and yours.

Success and the Expectations of the Team

When a group of people start out on a vocational adventure, each team member hopes that the success of the venture will in some way fulfill his or her personal dreams as well as fulfilling the commonly established goals. This fact contributes to a most intriguing dynamic which can emerge once success is reached.

During the building period, the entrepreneur-leader is seen, at least partially, as one who is using his or her own creative powers for the rest of the group—even though this may not be true and grossly selfish motives may prevail. The leader's aggressive use of power in overcoming common obstacles and people "blocking the way" are viewed by the team as a *good* use of power—just as a national leader's use of power and violence against the *enemy* in wartime is often seen as a good thing by the citizens of his country. This is true in the development of a company, even if everyone knows the leader is benefiting personally by power tactics—and perhaps more than anyone else.

But when success has been achieved, and the enterprise is established, suddenly the leader's use of power begins to be interpreted in an entirely different way. The same aggressive and almost ruthless driving of people and machines is resented, once the fear of defeat or failure has subsided.

During the Second World War, the American people submitted to gas and food rationing with a certain ease, but since the war we have resented *any* attempt to limit our consumption. And evidences of personal aggrandizement and the use of special privilege which were winked at during the war are now looked upon as unfair and arrogant. Dr. Paul Tournier has indicated that people consider aggressive or violent behavior as being "proper" if it is used in the service of others. But such behavior is seen to be "improper" when it is "violence on one's behalf, aimed at securing power for oneself, violence which is inspired by the fascination of power."*

Many entrepreneurs are baffled by what they interpret as "sudden disloyalty" on the part of their team members just as success seems to be assured. But it seems to me they fail to take into account the personal dreams of those who are on the venture with them. Just because the entrepreneur has accomplished his or her goal and reached his or her dream, it does not follow that the members of the team have achieved *their* goals. As a matter of fact, reaching the overall primary

---

* Paul Tournier, *The Violence Within* (New York: Harper & Row, 1978), p. 113.

goal merely *sets the conditions* for the others to know whether or not their goals are going to be reached.

For that reason, when the leader's primary goal has been achieved, I think it's a good time for him or her to have private conversations with all the team members regarding their personal vocational dreams. And if it's possible to help them visualize a way to reach their goals within the newly established venture, the overall attitude throughout the company or institution can be greatly improved.

Failure on the part of the leader to use the newly acquired success and power to help his or her teammates can appear to be a failure to care about the ones who "put you where you are." Bear in mind always that, when corporate goals are reached, the thirst for power among the team members may lead to all kinds of apparently unrelated conflicts over procedure. And these ego conflicts can be very confusing to the leader if he or she isn't aware that some of them may be oblique calls for attention and recognition.

The Entrepreneur's Family

The achievement of a major goal may also have a subtle effect on the family of an entrepreneur or innovator. The wife or husband may assume that, after all the time and energy poured into the cause have resulted in success, more attention can now be directed to the family. But as any entrepreneur knows, reaching the goal of establishing a large enterprise is only the beginning of the work.

I can certainly attest to the dangers that can threaten the marriage and family life of an entrepreneur at this and other points. And I now believe that attention needs to be given to one's family life at every point along the way. But perhaps the moment of peak achievement is precisely the time when very special attention should flow out to your spouse and family, to those who have supported you on the uphill climb.

Failure to give such attention may be interpreted by the family as a self-centered misuse of your newly obtained power. For a long time it did not occur to me that the power I receive in a business success might be a great threat to my wife. But in the face of a business success it would be easy for her to feel that I've "got it made" and don't need her the same way any more.

The point is: even though you as the leader of a business or institution that has become successful may not *feel* any different when it comes to your values and relationships, your success and newly acquired aura of power may affect other people's feelings toward you. And spending time tending and nurturing those relationships can be a major element in the development of a sound business or other enterprise—and a strong family.

This chapter is included here because I've been there! In the midst of my learning to use the creative enterprise process at BFI, my own family life disintegrated. And I began to ask myself some very important questions about my life and its frantic complexity—questions which in the long run may be a lot more important than achieving vocational goals.

PART THREE

A Better Quality of Living Through Creative Enterprise

Chapter 24

THE SEARCH FOR A CERTAIN QUALITY OF LIFE

At Browning-Ferris, I became acutely aware of the enormous power which can be released by a team of people who are on a common adventure and committed to a common cause. We had dreamed, set large goals, developed action plans, put together an experienced and highly motivated team, and made a serious commitment to reach our goals. And what happened exceeded all our expectations. There was a power and energy released among us which was more than the sum of our individual abilities and energies.

Physicists, I am told, speak of certain combinations of elements at a microcosmic level from which the resulting energy released is greater than the total that could be obtained by adding the separate, individually released energies together. This is called "synergism." And it seems to me that the creative enterprise process I have been describing produces synergistic effects which can be enormous in their potential—the joint results are greater than the sum of the individuals' abilities and efforts. And I think this synergism results partially from men and women being in positions which are "right" for them.

The Power of "Naturalness"

At BFI, as I watched people assigned to positions for which their natural abilities seemed to have prepared them all their lives, I began to see how a person's vocational life is enriched and enhanced by functioning in a position which appears to "fit" his or her natural abilities and desires. (This may account for my belief that it is important for people of any age to take the time to identify their true goals and then press forward to achieve them.) I noticed that, for people who felt they were in the "right place," there was a harmony and almost restful satisfaction in accomplishing the smaller tasks within the larger plans. And I began to see that "naturalness" was not only an attractive virtue, but a very valuable one.

The natural, synergistic atmosphere at BFI was very positive, and I felt good about my place there. But as I became more aware of what was happening, I started to feel restless and dissatisfied about some areas of my *personal* life—because there were elements there that did *not* feel natural.

Symptoms of Dis-ease

During the four years that BFI was aggressively acquiring other companies in the late sixites, I spent almost every day traveling. I would be in three or four different cities within a week's time. The hours were long; I would drink a lot of coffee, smoke cigars throughout the day, and eat a heavy dinner. I almost always had something alcoholic to drink, and I got very little sleep.

The things I went through during those years turned my life inside out in some ways. And while it isn't easy to go back over this in my mind, it somehow seems important to share these experiences with you.

After months of stressful living during the acquisition period, I began to feel sluggish and uneasy physically. I have always had a lot of energy. So when I felt sluggish, I'd just shake my head, to clear it, and go on. But finally the effects of that exhaustion which comes from intense mental and emotional effort—with no exercise and no time off—got to me.

I realized gradually that the way I was living and treating my body was anything but natural. And I was having to drive myself to overcome my physical "down" feelings. However much we were accomplishing as a company by the natural deploying of people and abilities, I was certainly not having any synergistic effects in my personal life. And I began to realize that, even if we built the biggest and best solid waste company in the world, any success we achieved really wouldn't matter if I didn't know how to live as a personally fulfilled human being. I knew that something had to change.

Diane and I had drifted so far apart by that time that a divorce, even though very painful, seemed to be the only answer. And so we were divorced.

But it was at this time, too, that I came to see it was senseless and impossible to keep crashing through my days and nights as I had been. And I began to get in touch with some of my feelings. I admitted to myself that I had gone downhill physically, and I began to feel a haunting need for a kind of simplicity which I'd always sensed could be found but which had always eluded me. I realized that I needed the courage to *live* and not just "respond to opportunities." Finally, I saw that I needed to take charge of my personal life the way I'd taken charge of my vocational life. I was becoming aware, in a way I didn't understand, that I yearned for a whole new quality of living.

Running, A First Step

At the time, of course, I didn't realize this with the clarity I'm describing it to you here. Outwardly, I feel pretty sure that I gave every appearance of being optimistic and successful. But the sedentary and overindulgant way of life had taken its toll. Something needed to be done. And then I realized that what my body was really craving was exercise.

One morning I decided to run, in order to shake off my lethargy. And I felt better. Then I made the decision to run regularly. I knew that I should begin gradually. And I'd start out walking in the early morning, breathing deeply and taking time to stretch. I'd walk until my body seemed to be ready to break into a very slow comfortable jog.

Sometimes I'd feel a few aches and pains, but as the blood

started to flow and my whole body gradually "woke up," the pains would dissolve. And as I increased my speed I found myself breathing faster and harder and felt that I was going to "run out of breath." But I learned that this is just a sign of the body's increased requirement for oxygen, that I should not let the fast breathing intimidate me, since I'd soon get over it.

After some months I started to vary the way I concluded my run. Sometimes I would go a little faster as I approached home. But I always ran at a comfortable pace, and, before stopping, I'd mix a little running with walking.

Gradually, over a period of weeks and then months, I increased the distance I was running without being consciously aware that it was happening. After a year or so, I was running five miles three or four times a week.

There is no way I can adequately describe the changes which began to take place in my life. As I was running, I started letting my mind wander and found myself dreaming creatively again. I didn't feel the need to solve a particular problem, but just let my thoughts range wherever they wanted to. Each day, running became a sort of small vacation from stress. And before many weeks had passed, the fuzzy, heavy sensations were gone, and I experienced a new surge of energy and alertness. I felt a new enthusiasm for life and for my work. At the same time, I became more sensitive to nature. While I was running I *saw* trees, the sky, animals. I even began to smell the earth and rain, after years of rushing through my days with sensory "blinders" on regarding nature. And I found myself caring more about the persons with whom I worked.

Just as I was beginning to notice the trees and grass and colors of the changing skies—which had been there all the time—I began to "notice" the persons who were living behind the faces at the office. A feeling of kinship with other human beings began to come through as I got in touch with my body through running.

Life became fun for me, and I came to see, as a result of my running experience, that for years my inner self had been crying out for a simpler way to live my whole life.

Moving Toward Simplicity

I know that it may sound idealistic and utopian to speak of simplicity in living while writing a book about the very complex and demanding creative enterprise process. But it was in the midst of our busiest time at BFI that I actually began to find a new way of life and to experience a new kind of "simplicity." This discovery went against everything I had ever felt before.

In April of 1973, Judy Hall and I were married. We were very much in love and I was determined to carve out more time for my family. Judy wanted a less frantic life too, but for a while she didn't know quite what to do with a man who was up before dawn running along the streets of Houston. But she liked the end results, because running made me a lot calmer. I was less restless, slept more soundly, and woke up more refreshed. And by the time I finished running each morning, I was in a much quieter mood to begin my working day. This began to change the pace and tone of the rest of my life. I wasn't *slower,* just not as *frantic.* I felt as if I could more nearly "decide" my decisions rather than "picking one hurriedly."

Then some things began to happen to me which were side effects of my exercise program. But they were in some ways just as important as the improved physical condition and emotional climate in my life. I realized that I was over scheduled, that I always felt I had more to do than I could handle in a day. Then I'd rush home in time to go out to some social function I didn't want to go to. Judy and I really enjoy time alone together, and we both needed more solitude. I yearned for a day to just read or walk on the beach, but there was never time.

A New Life—Using "The Process"

Finally, the brief tastes of simplicity I was experiencing were so much better than the "stress pool" life had been that I felt I *had* to find a way to simplify my whole life if I were ever going to be happy and enjoy the process of living. It was then

I realized that many elements of the creative enterprise process could be used to help me find a better, happier, and more productive quality of life.

I began to *dream* about what a simple life might be like for me. I knew that there were several major areas I needed to change in order to enjoy my own ultimate potential as a person. But I'd never had a definite way of planning to change my personal life.

Action Planning in "Real Life"

After I had run for a while I decided I wanted to run the Boston Marathon. My first attempt at reaching this goal was a fiasco. I finished among the last runners and had to walk the final ten miles to finish at all. For me, this was an extremely difficult experience. And I was embarrassed about my performance since a whole group of us went together from Houston to participate in the marathon. But as I cooled down after that race, I made an important commitment. First I set a goal: to run the Boston Marathon—all the way. When we got home, I created a training action plan and made the commitment. And beginning right after my first attempt to run the marathon, I started to watch my diet carefully. I don't think I ate any sweets for an entire year. My weight went from 197 pounds to approximately 177. And I trained assiduously.

Finally, in 1978, the day came to redeem myself. At the ten-mile point I was feeling intense pain. It seemed as if the hills along the course were getting steeper. I couldn't account for this because this time I had trained properly. But I closed my eyes and said to myself, "I am going to run until I fall." I really don't recall being conscious again until the twenty-one or twenty-two mile mark. I can remember a policeman on a loudspeaker saying, "You have now conquered Heartbreak Hill." I looked around, and the people I was running beside were much leaner than those I had been with at this distance the year before. Although there were dozens of runners faster than I, this was clearly a different group than I had run with previously.

All this time I was feeling a *lot* of pain, but I kept repeating, "I don't know what I am doing here or how I got this far, but I am going to run for that finish line." I finished the race in a very respectable time for me, a full two-and-one-half hours less than the year before.

After the race was over I realized two things: (1) I had shown courage in finishing in the face of the fear of failure, and (2) I could use the creative enterprise process in all sorts of ways in my personal life to do things which seemed impossible. While I didn't want to make running a highly competitive activity in my life, I now knew that with some structure I could do about what I wanted to physically.

At first I thought that applying the action plan techniques to physical and personal goals would only work for me because of my particular need for security and order. But then I watched a strange thing happen to my wife.

Up to that time, Judy hadn't been especially interested in running. I believe strongly that people should try to realize their own ambitions. So, after telling her how much better I was feeling since I'd started running, I never urged her to run.

But then, sometime in 1976, Judy decided on her own to begin running. The first day she could only go one hundred yards, but after a year she was able to run a mile. At that point she said, "I don't think I'll ever be able to run any farther. You know I flunked physical education." But she kept running a mile a day, and in time joined several other women who ran. They enjoyed the physical and emotional benefits from running, and began to talk about the different quality of living they were experiencing—of feeling more whole and complete.

Finally, Judy and a group of these women decided that they wanted to try to run a marathon. They set a goal, devised a specific action plan to increase their distances, and followed that plan religiously. And all of the women completed the 1978 Honolulu Marathon—twenty-six miles.

If you had asked Judy two years before about running a marathon, she would have laughed and said there was no way that was even possible. Judy's daughter, Jill, who was there to watch her mother cross the finish line, could hardly believe it herself. By setting a goal and establishing a specific action plan, Judy was able to accomplish that which appeared to be impossible for a homemaker with a teen-aged daughter.

As I watched Judy and her friends prepare for and run that race, I realized something very important in a new way. Our perception of how capable we really are is usually so colored by our fear of failure and our early inhibitions that most of us have no idea of real potential we *actually do* possess. And I saw that the creative enterprise process can help people discover and actualize personal as well as vocational abilities they've never even dared dream of.

As Judy and I got more involved with running, I realized that we had also entered a new world of people who were enjoying their lives and their bodies more than they ever had. I am certainly not recommending that everyone become a marathon runner. But the point of this story is that it is possible to set your own personal as well as vocational goals and to devise action plans to meet them. And as you do, you may discover the adventure of finding ways to improve the quality of every area of your life.

Like the entrepreneurial venture, the search for one's ultimate potential really begins with a commitment to dream about what life might be like for you. Then you can begin checking out your dreams in a reality-oriented way. And that can lead you toward a definite commitment and a whole new adventure of living.

Chapter 25

BEGINNING AN ADVENTURE OF LIVING

This adventure has no neat rules that I know of. For me it began all alone, at the point of my frustration with the quality of life I was experiencing. But I know now that the circumstances of beginning can vary widely for different people.

For instance, one day an outstanding Swiss banker friend, who had begun this search for a better quality of life, was riding with a client in a limousine in London. This client, who was one of the most successful international businessmen in the world, had been experiencing many of the symptoms of a stressful and overcrowded life, and he shared this frustration with my friend.

When he finished talking, the banker thought a few seconds, then put his hand on his client's arm, looked him in the eye, and said, "You can have anything money can buy and travel anywhere in the world you want to go. But I can give you something that will be a lot more important than anything you can buy or any place you can travel—if you want it." His client looked at him and realized that he was serious. "I'm very interested," the client said. "What are you talking about?"

"I can give you your health," the banker replied, "and perhaps an attitude which will be an important part of the foundation for a new kind of happiness."

The client said, "I'm ready now."

The Swiss banker, who is a very direct person, asked the driver to stop the limousine right where they were, beside a large public park in London. And in their business suits the banker and client went for a run in the park. From that time on, the client has continued a running and exercise program which had its beginnings that day in London—a program which has opened to him the search for a new quality of life.

A People With Enthusiasm for Living

As I began to meet people who had somehow gotten started running or jogging, I noticed that many of them were experiencing some of the same synergistic "side effects" I was, with regard to their attitude toward their families and personal lives. This change in attitude is difficult to explain. In my case, it was almost as if I'd gotten a new set of eyes. One day I had tunnel vision; I was only able to "see" and hear things having to do with BFI. Then, after I had been running a while, it was as if some shell—or perhaps the "tunnel"—had dissolved, and I began to see the people and events around me as well as my work. I felt much closer to Judy and the kids, for instance, and enjoyed times together with them. And I began getting interested in the process of living.

One day in 1973, after I had been running about three years, I visited Dr. Kenneth Cooper's aerobic center in Dallas, Texas. There, I met a group of men and women who were sharing their newly acquired state of health. They were sensitive, kind, and friendly as I asked questions and listened to what they said they were learning and enjoying. I recognized that these were busy business and professional people who were doing this for only one reason: what exercise did for them. But I could also feel a stimulating camaraderie and a sense of commitment to excellence as they shared the discoveries they were making. And they encouraged each other and me, even though I was a stranger.

As I watched these sharp people and listened to them laugh and talk and help each other, the thought kept coming to me: "This is the way creative people ought to relate." Many of them had responsible positions and worked very hard. But through the adventure to find physical health, they were learning how to "play" in a way that was healthy and re-creating.

On another occasion, I was participating in the 1978 Nike Marathon in Eugene, Oregon, and was at about the eighteen-mile mark when I came upon a wheelchair participant. Keep in mind that this fellow had gone the eighteen miles also, but in a wheelchair.* As I went by him, I am sure he could see that I was as tired as he was. Not a word passed between us, but on an impulse I pointed to myself and then to him, simply to indicate "I love you." I was about ten yards down the road when he yelled after me, *"Go for it!"*

And just those words, "Go for it!," from a man most people would call a cripple—who was "running" a marathon with his arms—seemed to change me somehow. I realized that, in approaching simplicity, I was beginning to discover something about the ultimate strength and *meaning* that is possible for a human being, regardless of his or her physical condition.

Changing Priorities to Get It Simple

As my need for simplicity grew, I came to see that I had no idea how to achieve such a goal. But I realized that I needed to include in my action plans for each year some concrete times, places, and experiences which would be conducive to simplicity and peace.

In business, I'd learned that important things just don't happen dependably if I don't spell them out as goals and include them in action plans. And now I was seeing that the same thing was true of my personal relationships and my quest for simplicity. If I didn't plan specifically, I'd never have time to experience the fullness of life I was beginning to taste.

Some Moves Toward a Simpler Life

Some of the activities we became involved in as a family to put "parentheses" of simplicity into our lives may not be

---

* Although some wheelchair "runners" are faster than many regular participants, they are often given an early start to avoid having the wheelchairs in the pack of runners at the starting line.

things other people would enjoy. But here are some that have helped us.

Judy and I were married in Carmel, California, a beautiful place with magnificent scenery. We made a commitment to go back each year and renew the simple vows we made to each other. Judy and I felt that in Carmel, in that atmosphere of simplicity and natural beauty, we would be able to take another step each year toward what we hope will be a long and successful marriage. And if for some reason we can't make it to Carmel some year, we'll find another beautiful place close to home.*

Another step we took to build simplicity into our lives was to invest in a beach house in Galveston, Texas, near the Gulf of Mexico, and to start going there at least one weekend a month when the weather was nice. We would play in the water with our kids, and feel the deep peace that comes to us with the salt water smells and the sound of the seagulls.

For me, it was always a beautiful experience to sit and watch the regular ebb and flow of the waves against the shore, to run in the edge of the surf and see the reflection of the sun and the clouds on the smooth, wet sand. And it was a thrill to listen to the steady pounding of the waves, like a healthy heart beating at the center of life. During these experiences I began to find myself thinking of God more often. I thanked him for a new chance at life and for all he's made, and asked him what it all meant and what I should do about my new discoveries.

A Day Off, Just for Me

Another thing I started doing in 1976 to help increase a sense of simplicity was to start taking "an ideal day off"—just for me—at a place where no one from the office could reach me.

* I am aware that many people do not have the same control of their time nor the financial resources to do the things I am describing. But it is amazing how many things people can do to simplify their lives—things which do not cost money or extended time.

I know that may sound very selfish, but a psychologist friend told me that it is important to occasionally do things like that if I want to have anything creative to give other people.

Such an ideal day for me would start with a morning run on the beach or through the woods for forty-five minutes or an hour. After the run I would shower and relax for a few minutes—and maybe even lie down again for a short rest. Following that, I might slip into my old jeans and enjoy a really good breakfast. And from there I would move through the day—writing, listening to music, reading. Later in the afternoon, I would take another run, and perhaps a short swim. Or at times I would enjoy just sitting on the beach and watching the surf. In the evening I would have dinner and maybe a conversation with friends and family. Then I would be ready to go to bed early.

Because there are other people in my family and because there are often unforeseen interruptions, it is not always possible to arrange for such a day off. But I have found that if I really give it priority, build it into my planning and/or combine it with an ideal day for my wife, it can sometimes happen—and the strength and personal renewal I feel as a result make it worth the trouble of scheduling it.

Day Is Done

Even though I was finding more and more ways to "get away" from my business periodically for times of rest and recuperation, I found I still had trouble "getting away" mentally. It seemed that I could never stop my mind from working. Then I remembered something from the time of BFI's rapid expansion that really helped me.

We had had a private plane, and one of the pilots taught me a principle which has helped me a lot. After landing in the city where we intended to stay that evening, he would reach into a beer cooler, pop the top off a can, take a big drink, and then say, "This plane is grounded." (A pilot cannot legally fly when he's had a drink.)

I started using a similar approach to business conversations and decisions at the end of each day. When it came time to shut down, I would stop as if there were a law against continuing to "fly" my business that day. And although there are many exceptions, much of the time I'm able to just walk away from the office.

Silence

Another thing which became important in my life (though difficult to come by) was a period of silence sometime during each day. Usually the ideal time for me was in the morning, when I was running. During this time I would often pray. And sometimes, after I ran and before I started my working day, I would take a few minutes to read a chapter of the Bible. I found the sense of peace I gained from these activities was worth the extra time they took.

Of course, it's not possible for a creative venturer to always be peaceful and relaxed in our kind of world. However, through taking these steps to simplify my life and allow for some solid rest and relaxation, I found that a certain peace could be achieved regularly. And this peace allowed for a rebuilding of the strength and energy necessary for the new challenges in my life.

Chapter 26

A COMMITMENT TO SIMPLICITY—AND THE COURAGE TO CHANGE

As I began to feel more healthy and at peace, I saw that unless I really made a *commitment to continue* trying to live a simple life, the surrounding jungle of demands and activities would recapture the small clearings I'd hacked out of my schedule. So I took a big step and made living simply a conscious goal for the rest of my life.

I had begun to realize that, when I made room for simple living, I found a new energy and enthusiasm welling up within me, and *a new clarity of judgment.* Even though I could operate under great stress during short periods in order to get certain things done, there would come a time when I would burn out and almost quit caring. This always seemed to occur when I was exhausted. And it was at such times that I was likely to make serious errors in judgment, and relationships with important people in my life were likely to be bruised or broken.

So I decided that, if I was thinking about staying in business for a long time, I would be much more productive if I worked out a relaxed rhythm in my personal life—rather than driving myself relentlessly day and night. All of this seems obvious now, and yet it took me almost forty years to begin to actually change the way I live.

An Outward Sign to Remind Me

Once I had made the commitment that, whatever it cost, I was going to make simplicity of life a real priority, I needed a concrete symbol of that fact—a continuing way to remind myself how fulfilling the simple things in life can be.

My car became that symbol for me. In 1971 I had bought a Chevrolet convertible. Since I had been fortunate in my business dealings, that was a rather modest car for me to drive. But I loved the feeling of freedom I had when I was at the wheel. Later, the car began to stand for the sort of openness I was feeling toward nature, people, and life itself.

As the years went by, I continued to drive that same car. And now, almost ten years later, when I'm driving that Chevy I am reminded how important simple living is to me. I am not criticizing the use of fine cars, which many people prefer. I have enjoyed driving expensive cars and riding in limousines, but my greatest personal satisfaction still comes in driving my 1971 Chevrolet. It has come to stand for a healthier, more peaceful life in the midst of an increasingly complex material jungle which presses in on us from all sides.

I don't know what other people might find to remind them to keep it simple. But I've needed that car so I won't take material success so seriously that I might abandon my commitment to personal meaning and hope.

Courage and Commitment

As I actually tried to change the way I live in response to my new commitment, I realized that it takes a certain courage to establish and maintain a simple lifestyle. How do you go about changing a life which has been so wrapped up in work that there has been no time or energy left for really living? This is an especially difficult question if a major portion of "after work" time is devoted to social obligations that aren't especially satisfying or renewing.

People have very different social tastes, but often a family never takes the time to question or evaluate their social activities. And I have become convinced that a simple lifestyle is impossible for any of us when we are controlled by extensive vocational and social obligations. Judy and I used to attend a number of big formal occasions. But as we evaluated our feelings, we decided that we really enjoy smaller, more personal groups. And we're both very happy when we can just be alone together or have some solitude doing what we enjoy.

But how does a person (or a couple) who has been caught up in the social rat race go about changing and simplifying a life style without offending people? How can this be handled without seeming to reject others and without feeling rejected ourselves? These are important questions because the fear of being rejected or of making people angry is often a major obstacle to having the courage to change.

There are other blocks as well. Many people fear they will lose their jobs or miss important promotions if they don't "make all the parties." This fear is especially acute for people who are managers (or married to managers) in corporations that seem to demand a great deal of business socializing.

These are not idle fears. The changes required when you decide to take your life goals seriously may be costly. But there *are* alternatives. Some people I know have talked to their bosses, describing their need to carve out some family time from their social schedule. And many have been surprised to find that extended socializing wasn't really expected.

Other people who wanted to make lifestyle changes have done some identifying of goals and looked for other jobs or vocational ventures which would allow them to make desired changes in their personal living. Since Keith and I started this book, several friends who were well-established vocationally—including his wife, Andrea—have quit their jobs and started new vocational adventures.

So often, because of our fear of failure and our inability to see our own real potential, we never even seriously *consider* changing our lives and trying to achieve our personal goals. But if simplicity, for instance, becomes a major focus, it may be possible that a social schedule can be arranged to work toward that goal.

Changing Routine Can Threaten Others

One relatively fast way to work toward greater simplicity is to alter one's daily routine. For instance, I have found it very restful to set the alarm earlier to give me time to run and start the day more slowly. Just one extra hour can become a lever which can lift and change a person's whole life.

But even a simple thing like starting to run daily or getting up early may take courage. Friends, and even one's own family, can be threatened by change. They may ridicule or reject you, or simply look amused in a superior way. A decision to become healthy and trim can be interpreted by your spouse as something more sinister—a dissatisfaction with the marriage or even an affair. So I believe it's a good idea, if you are looking for a simpler, healthier life, to thoroughly discuss your dreams with your whole family. A lack of understanding on their part can make it difficult to interrupt familiar habits and begin the adventure toward wholeness.

Where Does Courage Come From?

I realize you may be thinking that the reason I was able to simplify my life, as I have described it here, was that by the time I started trying I "had it made" and could relax. But the truth is that I have had to handle *more* stressful situations and have accomplished more in my vocational life than I did before I began this search. And as I have mentioned, at one point after I left Browning-Ferris I almost had to start over financially. But somehow, what I was discovering personally meant so much that—even when I was afraid—I found the courage to go after my dreams of simplicity.

But I began to wonder where that courage was coming from. I wondered what it was that would allow me or anyone else to take charge of feelings and act with courage despite the fear of failure.

In thinking this through, I remembered the courage I discovered in myself as I ran my second Boston Marathon, and I realized that courage had been the result of making an all-out commitment and working for a year to get in shape. I also remembered the courage which had come to me years before, when I made an all-out commitment to the Browning-Ferris project.

Then it hit me that maybe one source of courage to overcome

the fear of failure is a serious commitment of one's life to an important goal. I saw that when I began to dream about my personal life, to set goals and design realistic action plans, *then* I felt confident that achieving my goals was possible. I had made a serious and specific commitment of my life to achieve simplicity. And then, with God's help, I began to find the courage to change.

PART IV

USING CREATIVE ENTERPRISE TO SOLVE SOCIETY'S PROBLEMS

Chapter 27

DREAMING BIG

The last section of this book is by far the most frightening for me to write. I am afraid that, after hearing the dreams I want to share here, you will think I am naive about the complexity of large institutions and what can be done in and through them. So I want to say at once that I know "pouring concrete" to any of these dreams would take an enormous amount of creative dreaming, planning, and hard work on the part of many talented men and women. But very few people have presented *any* viable approach to the kind of problem-solving which might effect the changes that seem necessary today. So dream with me, with the understanding that these dreams *must seem* simplistic until we isolate specific goals and design action plans to meet them.

I feel a great frustration when I see some of the problems we are facing as a free society. The difficulties appear to be so numerous and complex that I'm often tempted to despair. But as I have experienced the power and efficiency of the creative enterprise process at work in business and in my own personal life, I have found a new hope. And I now believe it is possible to use this process as a way to create an astounding "power leverage" in dealing with complex human problems. By setting clear goals and breaking them down into do-able action plans, I believe some very significant changes can be brought about in our society. And I believe this can be done through specific ventures designed and run by relatively small squads of creative people.

Some Examples of Dreams and Projects

To begin with, let's say that one wanted to attack the problems of the *basic health and happiness* of entrepreneurs, innovators, and managers wherever they are found—in business, in the home, or in the helping or healing professions. How would one start to help such a powerful and independent group of people? How could they begin to discover their own full potential and perhaps together develop programs which might awaken America's healing energies?

Dream with me for a moment. What if there were a preventive medicine center where people could have their physical health evaluated by competent professionals. After these evaluations had been studied, nutritional and fitness experts could design concrete programs of fitness and diet tailored *specifically* to the executives' needs.

Then imagine a diagnostic kind of conference being offered at the same center by other competent professionals. At this conference the entrepreneurs and executives could examine the other areas of their lives in which they have difficulties that are blocking their personal fulfillment. This examination would take in, besides the medical, fitness, and nutritional areas, the emotional, financial, intellectual, and spiritual aspects of living.

For example, in the financial area, a man might discover that, although he is making a great deal of money, a lack of good planning is creating havoc in his financial life. Or perhaps a woman realizes that her emotional needs are not being met, and that she in turn is not meeting those of her family and close associates.

A conference or seminar program to explore and diagnose needs of these kinds could be extraordinarily helpful. And, as the next step, outstanding leaders could teach courses designed specifically for people seeking the fulfillment of their potential in any one of these (or other) areas. This would enable the man with financial problems to discover ways to identify and set new financial goals and action plans. And the woman with unmet emotional needs could get in touch with her feelings and learn to ask for and give emotional support. Then, as people began to find their ultimate strength in any one area, their whole lives could be energized. This often happens because, as a single part of one's life becomes bright and productive, there seems to be a natural tendency to want to look into other areas.

So here is my dream—a place with facilities for all these diagnoses and the working-out of the follow-up prescriptions and courses. Keep it in mind as we look at another dream.

Productivity

Many Americans are not aware that our country's percentage of growth in economic productivity has declined in the last few years. In fewer than ten years, if the trends aren't reversed, we could wind up falling from first in productivity to fifth or sixth—behind aggressive countries such as France, Canada, Japan, and Germany that are increasing their productivity dramatically.

So imagine with me a second center supported by industry—large and small businesses—where the problems of American productivity would be studied. At this center—and going out from it—would be specific educational programs designed to increase productivity. These programs would be produced by people who had made them work in specific industrial situations.

The Japanese have done absolutely amazing things by setting goals, doing action plans, and concentrating specifically on the problems of productivity in Japan. At an American center, the cross-fertilization of ideas and the dissemination of information could be synergistic beyond belief. And it could be done if only a hundred companies decided to make a minimum contribution each—and an entrepreneur took it on himself or herself to put it together.

As I said at the outset in this chapter, I know that some of you will think such dreams are impractical. But remember, in dreaming entrepreneurial dreams one does not encourage—or even tolerate—negative feedback during the dreaming or even the action-planning stages. I realize that *much* work would have to be done to flesh out any of these dreams. But here I only want to suggest some possible situations in which the creative enterprise process could be used in solving large social and economic problems. Later I will discuss some very concrete data.

Cumbersome Government Services

Here's another dream. In your imagination, picture one of the large and financially cumbersome government agencies. Imagine that you as an entrepreneur have seen an opportunity to run that agency as a profit-making venture. (I realize that an appropriate law or rule might have to be changed so private enterprise could take a shot at dealing with such a problem.) Of course, it would be more practical to start small, to tackle a problem in state or local government. But for the purposes of dreaming, let's take the national Social Security services (now under Department of Health and Human Services) for an example.

Let's say you see an opportunity to take the insured cases on the Social Security rolls and make a profitable business—an insurance company—with them. * Imagine going through the process of checking out the opportunity and the timing, setting major goals, breaking them down into minor goals, and doing action plans—which would take a lot of time but which certainly could be done and checked. I would bet almost anything I own that, by using the creative enterprise process carefully, a squad of entrepreneurs could not only make an efficient business out of Social Security but in the process could significantly improve many of its services to the public.

---

* This might mean that cases of noninsured people, like retarded children, for instance, would be handled by welfare. But in the process of examining the opportunity, goal-setting, and action planning, the whole program could be analyzed and the various functions clarified in terms of funding, cost, and efficiency.

This is the point at which I may lose some of you—by suggesting such a major project as Social Security. But one thing I have learned about the creative enterprise process is that *size* is not a deterrent if the other necessary ingredients (e.g., capital, experience, and timing) are present.

And if it were possible to revive Social Security into an efficient and profitable enterprise, then it might be true of many other areas in which the government is spending great sums of money with catastrophic financial results (e.g., energy control, ecology, etc.).

The question arises: why aren't entrepreneurs being given a chance to try? This is a complex issue—one reason is that many of the rules about the private sector not dealing with public problems are arbitrary and outdated. But another very important reason this situation hasn't been changed is that it is very difficult and cumbersome for creative people outside the legislative halls to have any continuing dialogue with lawmakers.

Entrepreneurs, innovators, managers, and educators, though often very powerful, are isolated from each other and are not often versed in how to communicate effectively with either "the government" or their fellow citizens. There is a lot of fear and suspicion on all sides. Businesspeople are suspicious of politicians (and vice versa). And the average educator or private citizen is suspicious of *both* business people (especially big business) *and* politicians. Real communication between these separated groups is almost nonexistent.

The power of government is centralized, and by comparison, monolithic. When a change of governmental policy or law is in the wind, the logistical difficulties involved in interested citizens getting together are very great. And since they don't get together, they can't agree, or get educated on what the real issues are, or suggest alternate ways to go. So the government often rolls on in awkward and inefficient directions, just from sheer momentum.

So in order for creative citizens to enter the decision-making process of the government in an effective and very powerful manner, there would have to be a way for them to get together quickly and efficiently, on very short notice, to instigate new actions as well as to understand and respond to changes in direction made by government officials and agencies. What kind of entrepreneurial dream could begin to solve this problem?

A Network of Creative People

One more time, let's do some dreaming. Imagine groups of a hundred members each—entrepreneurs, innovators, managers, educators, social workers, etc.—in each of the hundred largest cities in America. Imagine that these men and women are concerned about productivity and efficiency in government. And, although this dream sounds utopian, imagine that they are committed to a better quality of life for themselves, their families, and the rest of society.

Now, what if these groups belonged to a creative association in which they could work toward their common goals? (Remember, we are dreaming now. So no negative "it can't be dones" allowed at this point.)

Imagine that in each of these hundred cities there is the capability for a closed-circuit television network. Then, when a crisis occurs or a government change is proposed, all members across the nation could be notified in a few hours, by telephone or telex message, to meet at their local meeting place at a certain time. Then imagine that, at some central place in one city the men and women who are most knowledgeable about the proposed change are brought together to give the members of all these entrepreneurial groups a common private briefing over the closed-circuit network. The technology is currently available to do this in such a way that members in the various cities could ask questions of the television panel at the time of the briefing.

Imagine the effect which could be generated almost instantly by the representatives of *ten thousand American businesses, educational institutions, and social institutions* expressing opinions to Washington at the same time on any given issue. Overnight, the government would become accountable in a way it has never been.

This network could have access to programs designed to promote a better quality of life as well as to work at solving the problems of society. Members of such groups could learn how entrepreneurs and other interested citizens can influence public opinion by speaking in colleges, universities, high schools, and other institutions. Entrepreneurs, innovators, and managers could learn how to communicate with members of the press rather than hiding from them behind an ominous "no comment."

In short, through such a network creative individuals could have an enormous synergistic effect politically, educationally, and socially—as well as in their own lives. An organization such as we have imagined here would be a powerful tool for helping people in our free society find and exercise their own potential and ultimate strength.

I realize it sounds too easy on paper. And of course it would not be easy. But this is the wonder of the dreaming process: we can see an idea develop to completion. If we were allowed to shoot barbs at this point—before doing an action plan—we would never find out if this dream were in fact "do-able" or not. We could immediately say, "Oh, no, a super lobby!" or "Where would the money come from?" But if we set concrete goals to meet a real need in the free enterprise system and then did an action plan, we might be amazed to find that there are ways such a dream could be implemented.

Making Dreams a Reality

The four dreams I have just mentioned—a center for promoting a better quality of life among entrepreneurs and managers, a catalytic institution for the study and improvement of American productivity, a forum and information network for the participation of creative citizens in dealing with the country's changing problems, and a system for reforming unwieldly government agencies through the application of the creative enterprise process—all these are real dreams. They are ideas that began to take shape in my mind and in the minds of men I knew as I was thinking about ways to apply the principles that were reshaping my own life to some of the larger problems I could see around me.

As I considered the possibility of using the creative enterprise process as a tool to begin to isolate goals and work on some of the complex difficulties I saw, I was deeply moved. I began to believe that some of us who have benefited most from the free enterprise system have an obligation to try to see if we can't use the processes which have made this country great as a means of bringing a new wave of life and health back into it. But that meant going beyond the dreaming stage. In the next chapter I want to trace how, through the process we've been discussing, one of these dreams has become a reality.

Chapter 28

THE LAUNCHING OF A DREAM—THE HOUSTONIAN

As I began to put together in my mind what had happened to me personally—which had led me to reexamine and restructure my whole life—I got very excited. In the midst of the personal chaos and stress of modern life, could other burned-out, exhausted men and women and their families discover ways to reenergize and redirect their lives? And if we could start on a realistic adventure toward personal health and happiness, could we make it available to other people? Could some of us on the adventure use the creative enterprise process itself to feed this way of living into the veins and arteries of America?

I started to put together several things which had been developing in my mind: (1) I saw a great need everywhere I traveled in America and in Western Europe for a better, more healthy quality of living in the midst of affluence. I saw the need for physical well-being, simplicity, and some measure of peace. (2) I recognized the power of the creative enterprise process. This process had allowed me and a creative team, in a very few years, to change the face of an entire major industry which is essential to the survival of a metropolitan culture. (3) I knew that a revolution had taken place in my own life, health, and relationships. Because of the adventure I had begun through a commitment to running, I was finding a more satisfying and productive way of living in all areas of my life.

I realized I wanted to get with other men and women, rich or poor, who were discovering the same hope and sense of change I was beginning to find. And I started imagining that perhaps a group of us might use the creative enterprise process to establish a place, a center, where we could dream together and do something concrete about our own lives and about the future of the American system.

It was quite a fantasy—almost outlandish. But I couldn't shake the feeling that I was recognizing really significant needs that weren't being met anywhere. I felt that my idea held one of the few possible options I'd seen to get together the people with the strength and know-how to put new life and direction into society.

When I began to share my dream confidentially with a few friends, I found they could understand the problems I was identifying and relate to the direction I wanted to take. My friends whose lives were being changed through physical fitness programs like running and swimming were especially interested in the project, although at first building a center of the kind I envisioned sounded like such a large venture no one wanted to get too involved in it.

Setting Goals

As my dream became more and more real and important to me, I went about setting goals for a new project, which I had decided to call The Houstonian.

When I first began this process, I envisioned two primary objectives: (1) to help executives and professional people and their families discover and develop the highest quality of personal life and health possible, and (2) to provide a place where entrepreneurs, innovators, managers, and others who are concerned about the renewal of our free society could meet and begin to dream together. They could isolate specific projects and goals for revitalizing the free enterprise system and the major institutions in it.

I realized that building a center with such goals would demand not only a strong commitment, but a deep trust in the historical timing of starting such a venture. The dream of doing this was so clear that I felt I had to try, regardless of the apparent material odds against such a center's succeeding at that time.

It was as if I had been told to stand up, and when I did I found I was on a surfboard. And as I looked around I sensed that I was on a huge historical wave of concern about the renewal of individual life and of our free society. My job then was not to furnish the power. My job was to keep my balance and bring together every skill and resource I could in order to ride this wave as far as it might go out over American life.

A Center for Personal Renewal

But those feelings were only experienced by me in the privacy of the dreaming stage. As I got into the action plan, I began to see that, because of its size and complexity, the venture had to be a cooperative one.

I wasn't just thinking about personal renewal in terms of a physical fitness revolution—although that seemed essential to me. I was thinking about total lives. Through my own awakening and my conversations with people in different disciplines, I had come to realize that personal renewal may begin for different people through stress or awakening to needs in different areas of their lives.

In my case, my bad physical condition and sluggishness had made me aware that I was missing something and finally drove me to get some exercise. But other people I was meeting, who had begun the adventure toward personal renewal, had experienced *emotional* crises or blocks in relationships. Others had been confronted by *financial* failure—or surprisingly, by financial successes and the emptiness which followed.

Some people had been surprised by serious *medical* problems—heart attacks, strokes, cancer—and had to rethink their lives. And some had been confronted with weight problems or other *nutritionally-related* illnesses. Other people had simply realized that life was going by and they were not learning anything; their *minds felt stagnant* and they realized that they hadn't read or studied anything of substance outside their vocational field since they'd left school. Still others realized they were living in a *spiritual vacuum.* The narrow or formal religion of their childhood had been rejected but there was no new center of meaning and value to replace it. And finally, some got interested in personal renewal simply because they wanted to become all they could be and *fulfill their potential.*

I was excited as we gathered experts in different fields (medical diagnostician, nutritionist, physical fitness consultant, financial counselor, intellectual leader, spiritual counselor, psychological counselor, and others) at an action planning meeting. I saw that, regardless of which of these "doorways" one came through into the search, he or she was soon seeing needs in *other* areas of life. We all became fascinated as we saw the potential growth for our own lives in the accomplishments and expertise of the others.

For instance, one man had come into the renewal adventure because of a spiritual and emotional crisis and awakening years before. But as we talked about the dream for a center and how we'd gotten into it, he soon realized that he was out of shape physically and that he was not handling his finances well. After a medical examination and an exercise and nutritional prescription, his whole life began to change drastically over the next few months.

This man had always repressed the financial side of his life—feeling panicky if he didn't make enough money but guilty if he made "too much." So his finances were in a mess, even though he made a more than adequate living. After several months, he had a session with the financial counselor and began to set goals and get the necessary financial structure and discipline in his life.

At that point this man and his wife became so excited about the program we were developing that they agreed to become the first guinea pigs to check out *in their own lives* for a year all the major areas we'd been looking at. And as a result of the new sense of life and renewal they have already experienced, Keith Miller put aside his own schedule and is writing this book with me.

Financing and Building

At first I thought of trying to finance The Houstonian project through a charitable foundation. But almost at once I realized that, as interested as people say they are in a new idea, the contributing of really large sums of money is a different matter.

My financial investigation indicated that we were talking about approximately $39 million for the construction, initial staffing, and start-up of the center. And a brief investigation made it apparent that funding The Houstonian as a charitable venture would take entirely too much time.

I was disappointed that more people didn't come forward to help fund the project. Then it occurred to me that I'd been given this opportunity in the first place because of my successful use of the creative enterprise process. And if the needs we wanted to meet through the new venture were valid needs in society, then I believed those needs represented a legitimate entrepreneurial opportunity. So I decided to make the whole venture a traditional business deal.

I can imagine the thoughts of my associates and financial advisors as I told them I wanted to build a $39 million "conference center" which would not only be self-supporting but make a profit. But I made the investigations concerning the financial needs, possible income streams, experienced people I would need, location and building requirements, etc. I drew up action plans, and with a team I had been gathering, checked them. And when I saw that the dream had a landing field in the real world, I was ready to commit myself to it with everything I had.

Remarkable Timing Breaks

As at BFI, the series of "breaks" which happened when we began to translate our dream into a reality seemed almost miraculous.

As a part of the action plan I had located a twenty-acre wooded tract in the midst of the "magic circle" area of Houston. It had been owned privately and had several beautiful estates on it. The hundred-foot high pine trees on the tract were so numerous that from the streets surrounding the area no one could see into the property. There was easy access to two airports and downtown Houston.

It was a perfect site for a center like the one we were planning, but it appeared to be unavailable for commercial use. The owners had been adamantly set against such a sale. Just at that time, however, one of the principal owners became very interested in the ideas behind our wanting to build the center. With his help, we were able to purchase the twenty acres just when we needed it.

Another obstacle confronting us was the problem of obtaining the financing necessary to construct the project. At that time we did not have experience in the real estate development field. It's fairly obvious that this is a sizable loan for someone without real estate background to get. But we ultimately received a $30 million commitment from a major insurance company. That loan's coming through under the circumstances it did made me feel even more that what we were doing was part of an even bigger plan than we had in mind.

But there was still another money problem. A substantial amount of equity was required to complete the whole project. We made arrangements to borrow several million dollars from a bank. And at the exact time in our planning when a source for the balance of the equity was necessary, we were introduced to our current partner. For several years he had experienced a growing interest in preventive medicine and fitness. He was, in fact, the man who had been introduced to running by his Swiss banker friend in London. When we met in the summer of 1977, we felt an immediate rapport and a great deal of mutual confidence. The end result was that he agreed to supply a large part of the equity, which would allow us to go on with the building of The Houstonian.

That crowning piece of timing (or luck, or destiny) marked the end of our action planning stage. It was the moment to move forward. And so, with a great deal of excitement and a prayer for guidance, I made the big commitment and we began the building of The Houstonian.

As I write these words, I realize that the business venture I am describing may not sound unusual to some readers. But any entrepreneur who has tried to get a project of this size together will know how rare it is to have a virtual stranger be so motivated by the same dream you have that he puts up several millions of dollars for immediate financial needs.

The Gathering of People and Resources

During all this time I was meeting people in the most unexpected places and situations. These were men and women who also felt the need for personal renewal and who had been very disturbed about the apparent signs of decay in the free enterprise system. They came out of the woodwork with ideas, introductions to key people who could help with the medical program, the physical fitness center, or the management of the three-hundred-room hotel and conference center. I had the strange quiet assurance that we were indeed involved in an idea which was coming of age just as we were building a place for it.

In January of 1980, The Houstonian had its formal opening. There is a preventive medicine center where more than three thousand men and women have already had complete physical examinations at the rate of one hundred fifty to two hundred per month.* These people have been given specifically tailored nutritional and physical fitness programs to get their bodies in the best condition possible.

To further the goal of personal renewal, the Houstonian Foundation, a not-for-profit entity, is supporting programs at The Houstonian designed to help people who are already succeeding in some areas of their lives locate areas they want to work on to find their maximum potential health and happiness.

---

* The Preventive Medicine Center opened in 1978 at a different location in Houston to work out its operations and get its staff well-organized and experienced in The Houstonian approach before the Houstonian buildings were completed.

Chapter 29

AN EXPLOSION OF DREAMS

The launching of The Houstonian represented the fulfillment of one of my biggest dreams. But at the same time other dreams were being launched by people who had also caught the spirit of creative renewal around the Houstonian project. The story of how these dreams took shape is like the unfolding of the plot in a fascinating drama.

American Productivity

As I have mentioned, I originally envisioned The Houstonian as more than a personal renewal center. I saw it as a place for dreaming about the renewal of the free enterprise system—a launching pad for using the creative enterprise process to address institutional problems which have caused many people to despair about America.

In thinking about this second goal for The Houstonian, I saw that the creative agendas would come from people who were concerned about different aspects of society. Our job would be to provide ways to understand the use of the various creative enterprise processes, and to provide a context in which people could begin to meet and find ways for getting things done.

This is still a major focus of my dream for The Houstonian. But before I had even gotten an action plan started on that goal, I ran into a friend, Jack Grayson. Jack had been dean of the graduate business school at Southern Methodist University. He had had an illustrious career in economics—including being chairman of the Price Commission and consultant to the comptroller general of the United States. At this time, in 1976, Jack was working, writing, and lecturing with major industrial groups on problems connected with productivity.

Jack pointed out to me that there was a groundswell need for a focused approach to the symptoms of declining productivity in American industry. There was really no place where major industries could come and work in a cooperative way, with each other and with labor unions, on their shared problems and the challenges of increasing productivity.

Jack wanted to build a "productivity center" for this purpose—like the one I described in chapter 26. At the time, we were just designing our action plan for The Houstonian, and it soon became evident that the productivity center Jack was dreaming of needed to be a separate place.

The center would be financed, Jack hoped, by contributions from participating companies. He pointed out that the Japanese had built a similar productivity center in the 1950s, and that many Japanese economists and industrialists attribute much of that country's astounding national increased productivity to that center. Interestingly, it was built with several millions of American dollars.

At that time, Jack and I were both finding great renewal through a running program. We shared a lot of the same dreams for the renewal of corporate and personal life, and we were both involved in the process of tackling the problems beneath the symptoms in the free enterprise system. So, as I turned back to building The Houstonian, Jack began to set goals and design plans for a productivity center.

When he was ready to commit to developing the American Productivity Center, we set aside two acres of the twenty-acre Houstonian tract, and with the donations of one hundred of the major corporations of America * Jack launched this seven-

* The following is a partial list of corporations who contributed to the launching of the American Productivity Center: Alcoa Foundation, American Can Company, American General Companies, American Telephone & Telegraph Company, Anheuser-Busch, Inc., Armstrong Cork Company, Arthur Anderson & Co., Atlantic Richfield Foundation, Bank of America, Benjamin Franklin Sav-

teen million dollar center—a venture which is separate from The Houstonian but connected to it physically.

Since it opened in 1978, the American Productivity Center has been involved in creating a national awareness of the seriousness of our declining productivity. Many of the eighty employees are engaged in research and in seeing what different outstandingly productive companies (and countries) are doing to increase productivity. This information is disseminated through seminars (almost one hundred in 1980) and by consulting arrangements with different companies (about $700 thousand in consulting fees in 1980 and $1600 thousand for 1981).

The center interfaces with the legislators in Washington and gets information out about any legislation which might affect productivity. And, among other things, representatives of labor and management come together at the center to investigate ways in which they can cooperate to increase productivity.

It's hard to believe what has already happened through the American Productivity Center, which it seems was formed just as the problem of declining productivity has come to the national consciousness in such a powerful way in the automobile business and in other major industries.

---

ings Association, Browning-Ferris Industries, Inc., Caterpillar Tractor Co., Celanese Corporation, The Chase Manhattan Bank, N.A., Cities Service Company, The Coca-Cola Bottling Co. of New York, Inc., Continental Illinois National Bank & Trust Co., Corning Glass Works, Dana Corporation Foundation, Dresser Foundation, Inc., Eli Lilly and Company, Exxon Company, U.S.A., Fluor Corporation, Ford Motor Company, General Electric Company, General Foods Corporation, General Mills, Inc., General Motors Corporation, Gulf Oil Foundation, Halliburton Company, Hallmark Cards, H. J. Heinz Company, Hughes Tool Company, International Business Machines Corporation, International Harvester, International Telephone & Telegraph Corporation, Kaiser Aluminum and Chemical Corporation, Kraft, Inc., Lone Star Steel Company, Motorola Inc., J. C. Penney Company, Inc., Phillips Petroleum Company, Price Waterhouse & Co., The Prudential Insurance Company of America, The Quaker Oats Company, Ralston Purina Company, Reading & Bates Corporation, R. J. Reynolds Industries, Inc., Rockwell International, Shell Oil Company, Southwestern Mutual Life Assurance Company of America, Sun Company, The Superior Oil Company, Tennaco Inc., Texas Instruments Incorporated, Texas International Airlines, Inc., Time Incorporated, United States Steel Corporation, Westinghouse Electric Corporation, Weyerhaeuser Company.

The American Leadership Forum

Still another dream began to take shape about the time I was making plans for The Houstonian. Joe Jaworsky, an attorney who at that time was investigating The Houstonian concept with us, told me one day that he was deeply concerned about the lack of knowledge on the part of the average citizen (and particularly the average business and professional person) concerning the way change takes place in the American government and the free enterprise system. He was interested in the possible ways creative change might be fomented in the system, and in ways educational material and crucial information about change might be disseminated.

Joe spoke about the need for a network of people in different businesses and professions in the major cities of America, and he described a project much like the one in the dreaming section of chapter 26.

At that time, Joe was a partner in a large international law firm, and was in charge of that company's London office. But as his dream matured he began to set goals and design an action plan. Then, in the fall of 1980, Joe Jaworsky resigned his position in London and came to Houston to begin the formation of the American Leadership Forum, a network of men and women who are concerned with understanding and renewal in the free enterprise system.

As I am writing these words, Joe and his associates have already checked the action plan, have raised a substantial amount of the $2700 thousand start-up capital in a not-for-profit foundation, and are contacting interested people in various cities across the country. They are providing a "place" for creative men and women to come together who want to be a part of a powerful force for renewal in our society.

A Personal Dream for America

For several years I have had the feeling we may be overlooking the role that private enterprise has already played in establishing a free society. At The Houstonian, I am becoming increasingly aware of the power of some of the creative ideas of people like those of you who are reading these pages. In fact my hope in writing this book is that together some of us can actually do concrete things to help breathe healing new life and energy into the free society that we still have today. I pray that, as more of us decide to commit to this effort, our actions will be in the best interest of all people in free societies, because I'm deeply convinced that the creative enterprise process can be used to solve some of the most fearful social and governmental problems, as well as business ones.

Recently I have become aware again that the founders of this country were pioneers, dedicated to conquering new frontiers. There are no geographical frontiers in America now. But I believe that the entrepreneur and innovator represent the contemporary examples of those men and women who carved out an existence and a quality of life unequaled anywhere in the world. The entrepreneurs and innovators I am writing to in this book are those who can identify with the gutsy, risking heritage left us by those early pioneers.

How many times have you heard the phrase with regard to a creative venture that an American dream has come true. The "American dream" has a certain ring to it all around the world. And here in America that dream is still very much alive and is being achieved by people living today.

But the U.S. leadership role—economically as well as politically and militarily—is being tested. We in America represent the current hope for a free society. Investment dollars are coming to this country in very large amounts. Many foreign investors are of the opinion that we have another twenty years left in our current system. The reason given for coming here is that these investors want to invest as long as possible in a free and stable environment. And with all our restrictions, we are still by far the freest and most stable major nation in the world.

For the last few years I have had a great deal of opportunity to deal with foreign businessmen. I've seen a certain dimension in these people for which I was not prepared. Many of them have voiced a strong and passionate love for the American kind of freedom. During conversations you can almost feel them inhale the freedom which so many of us take for granted. They want very much for us to pull ourselves together and lead the world in a renewal of freedom in society. They're disturbed that our current focus seems to be on consuming television programs, autos, movies, and hamburgers—and apparently ignoring the health of the underlying system which produces them. To the extent this is true, I believe we are incredibly insulated from the seriousness of the real threats to our way of life.

It's been thirty-five years since the Second World War, which is the last time we in America were totally caught up in and committed to a really significant common cause. I think the Iranian hostage crisis reminded us somehow of how much we long to be together again as a people. There is a sense in which many have begun to lose faith in America. In response, some people say that we Americans are extremely resourceful, and of course this is true. But I feel that this resourcefulness could possibly slip away. I have wondered if it will take another World War to wake us up. And then would it be too late?

The reason I'm making these comments is that I believe many of us are in the process of getting fed up with our recent performance as a nation and as individuals. I think we are possibly entering an era of significant change and renewal. And I believe the entrepreneur-innovator could be the answer for the leadership necessary to revive our current private enterprise system and a free society.

I am not condemning all major institutional or governmental executives; many of these people are extremely resourceful. Many of them are really change-agent entrepreneurs. But a great many others seem to have the bureaucratic disease of being interested only in preserving what they have. They may deserve some of the criticism for greed and social irresponsibility that we in the business community receive—though there seems to be in all of us an unwillingness to take risks for others.

But I believe that entrepreneurs and innovators may have to take on the battle of rebirthing personal freedom and private enterprise, if it is going to be done. Think it over. Whom do you know who's going to work seriously at this? There are many forces acting to destroy our current system, some intentional and others unintentional. To turn things around, some people will have to get their personal finances in shape and commit one, five, ten years to specific ventures designed to produce creative change.

I believe some of us owe it to the system which has nurtured us to put something of ourselves back into it. Goals will have to be set, action plans drawn, and commitment decisions made by creative people. If individuals with the spirit of creative enterprise do find a way to stand and work together, there will be quite a contest—and quite an historically significant adventure. I pray to God that we at The Houstonian will provide one place where this adventure can begin for a few. And I hope some of you who read this book will join us . . . with no fear of failure.

THE BOTTOM LINE: AN EPILOGUE

—Tom Fatjo, Jr. and Keith Miller

Whether you are an entrepreneur interested in large dreams, a homemaker going through the midlife blahs, or a young person deciding what you would like to do with your life, we hope the creative enterprise process will give you some of the new hope and enthusiasm we're finding—for life and for the future of America and the free enterprise system.

These are exciting times for those who can dream and who have the courage and desire to follow those dreams through goals, action plans, and commitments.

The world is full of cynics and pessimists—and there *is* plenty to be concerned about. But those who only complain and criticize cannot dream the positive dreams on which a healthy future can ride into the present.

We believe in the combination of courage and creativity out of which the free enterprise system was forged. And we also believe that powerful innovators and entrepreneurs can be people of gentleness and sensitivity who can care about the poor and dispossessed. And since we know that the process we have described in this book has incredible power to make dreams come true, our prayer is that you, and we, will use it wisely.